NEW YEARS
SEAL DREAM

Bone Frog Brotherhood Book 1

SHARON HAMILTON

This is a work of fiction. Names, characters, places, brands, media, and incidents are either the product of the author's imagination or are used fictitiously. In many cases, liberties and intentional inaccuracies have been taken with rank, description of duties, locations and aspects of the SEAL community.

SHARON HAMILTON'S BOOK LIST

SEAL BROTHERHOOD SERIES
Accidental SEAL (Book 1)
Fallen SEAL Legacy (Book 2)
SEAL Under Covers (Book 3)
SEAL The Deal (Book 4)
Cruisin' For A SEAL (Book 5)
SEAL My Destiny (Book 6)
SEAL Of My Heart (Book 7)
Fredo's Dream (Book 8)
SEAL My Love (Book 9)
SEAL Brotherhood Box Set 1 (Accidental SEAL & Prequel)
SEAL Brotherhood Box Set 2 (Fallen SEAL & Prequel)
Ultimate SEAL Collection Vol. 1 (Books 1-4 / 2 Prequels)
Ultimate SEAL Collection Vol. 2 (Books 5-7)

BAD BOYS OF SEAL TEAM 3 SERIES
SEAL's Promise (Book 1)
SEAL My Home (Book 2)
SEAL's Code (Book 3)
Big Bad Boys Bundle (Books 1-3 of Bad Boys)

BAND OF BACHELORS SERIES
Lucas (Book 1)
Alex (Book 2)
Jake (Book 3)
Jake 2 (Book 4)
Big Band of Bachelors Bundle

TRUE BLUE SEALS SERIES
True Navy Blue (prequel to Zak)
Zak (Includes novella above)

NASHVILLE SEAL SERIES
Nashville SEAL (Book 1)
Nashville SEAL: Jameson (Books 1 & 2 combined)

AUDIOBOOKS
Sharon Hamilton's books are available as audiobooks narrated by
J.D. Hart.

ABOUT THE BOOK

Tucker Hudson has been off SEAL Team 3 for nearly ten years. He reluctantly attends his former Teammate's wedding on New Years Eve, vowing to keep his hands to himself and his mouth shut. Suffering nightmares from a tragic deployment, he barely left the Teams with an honorable discharge. Romance is one complication he does not need. And no one needs him either: not the Teams, not his family.

Brandy Cook knows she isn't as attractive as the skinny blondes who usually attend SEAL weddings. Although she's dieted for three months straight, she's only managed to fit into a size 16 dress, and only then with the help of a monstrous undergarment that nearly prevents her from breathing. So when the big grey-haired former SEAL with a body built like Shrek takes a passing interest in her, she figures he's been forced by a wager or some kind of trick.

But as the clock strikes midnight, the improbable happens and suppressed passions take over, ending in a steamy night neither will forget, but both will admit later was a huge mistake. When Brandy finds herself in trouble, Tucker turns out to be the only one who can keep her safe from the fury building around her world.

Book #1 of the Bone Frog Brotherhood.

AUTHOR'S NOTE

I always dedicate my SEAL Brotherhood books to the brave men and women who defend our shores and keep us safe. Without their sacrifice, and that of their families—because a warrior's fight always includes his or her family—I wouldn't have the freedom and opportunity to make a living writing these stories. They sometimes pay the ultimate price so we can debate, argue, go have coffee with friends, raise our children and see them have children of their own.

One of my favorite tributes to warriors resides on many memorials, including one I saw honoring the fallen of WWII on an island in the Pacific:

> "When you go home
> Tell them of us, and say
> For your tomorrow,
> We gave our today."

These are my stories created out of my own imagination. Anything that is inaccurately portrayed is either my mistake, or done intentionally to disguise something I might have overheard over a beer or in the corner of one of the hangouts along the Coronado Strand.

I support two main charities. Navy SEAL/UDT Museum operates in Ft. Pierce, Florida. Please learn about this wonderful museum, all run by active and former SEALs and their friends and families, and who rely on public support, not that of the U.S. Government. www.navysealmuseum.org

IF YOU GOT ANY CLOSER, YOU WOULD HAVE TO ENLIST

I also support Wounded Warriors, who tirelessly bring together the warrior as well as the family members who are just learning to deal with their soldier's condition and have nowhere to turn. It is a long path to becoming well, but I've seen first-hand what this organization does for its warriors and the families who love them. Please give what your heart tells you is right. If you cannot give, volunteer at one of the many service centers all over the United States. Get involved. Do something meaningful for someone who gave so much of themselves, to families who have paid the price for your freedom. You'll find a family there unlike any other on the planet. www.woundedwarriorproject.org

CHAPTER 1

"**N**O THANKS NEEDED, Tucker. I didn't ask you to be part of the wedding party because I didn't think you'd fit into a 5X tux on top with your XL waist. You're an action figure, Tuck. Besides, you drool."

Tucker growled as he turned his back on the groom, Brawley Hanks. The dressing room full of handsome penguins grunted and politely guffawed, since they were all dressed up and on good behavior.

"And there's no room for even a Barbie on his arm. Damn those church aisles," barked Riley Branson.

Another former Teammate, T.J. Talbot, grabbed Tucker's arm and drew him out of the Room of Doom, as the single SEALs called it. "Pay no attention to them. They're assholes. Also, who wants to walk down the aisle with a Barbie Doll?" He winked at Tucker.

He felt at ease immediately. Tucker's huge hands and fingers knotted themselves to oblivion, having no place to hide and looking like a bushel of antlers he was carrying. "Thanks, T.J. I hate these things," he said, pulling on his lapel. "But I've been out of commission so long, thought it would be nice to see some of the guys."

"And now you've seen that nothing has changed." T.J. was nearly as tall as Tucker, perhaps an inch shorter. He bumped foreheads. "But the girls will be younger because of Dorie, and that's probably a good thing," T.J. whispered.

"You having regrets, you old married fart?" Tucker murmured back.

Brawley's dad appeared in the church hallway before T.J. could answer and slapped both the former Teammates on the back simultaneously. "Glorious day, isn't it?"

Tucker knew old man Hanks was relieved his son had finally settled down and picked somebody. Brawley had more breakups than a pre-teen homeroom class.

"Yessir. Just took the right woman." T.J.'s face was shriveled up, like his last comment had soured his tongue. Tucker knew he was lying through his teeth. Privately, he thought, it took more alcohol than could fill a battleship to convince Brawley it was time to man-up.

"Dorie's a real nice gal," Tucker offered up. "You're gonna be a lucky father-in-law. She should fit in well with the rest of the family," he added, trying to keep a straight face. He knew it would be painful for T.J.

Both gentlemen looked back at him, T.J. not showing an ounce of expression. Mrs. Hanks was raised in the local Mennonite community. She was as plain as a saltine cracker, without any makeup or hair curling or adornments. Her two daughters were younger, even paler copies of her. Whereas Dorie looked like she could handle a Las Vegas pole and entertain a whole room of men. Those were going to be some interesting family dinners during the holidays, Tucker figured.

When he had the courage to look back into Mr. Hanks' eyes, he realized old man Hanks married her probably because little Brawley was on his way, and for no other reason. He felt the man's pain.

"You believe in miracles, son?" Hanks said, his eyes folded into thin slits.

"Yes, sir, I do. I surely do. That and redemption, too."

T.J. cleared his throat. "Well, congrats, sir. Must be a load off to have Brawley settled. I think those two will be happy together."

The far away look Mr. Hanks gave them back was difficult to read. Tucker had been feeling a little lonesome and sorry for himself until he encountered Hanks Sr. today. Now he was damned pleased he'd never hooked up with anyone.

Sure, they're pretty, but they're dangerous. Unpredictable. Who needs them? Certainly not me!

At last, Hanks pushed through the two younger men, heading for greener pastures, having exhausted any thought process he was following. He turned his head back to them and whispered, "Happiness' got nothing to do with it. All a state of mind, gentlemen." His fingers pointed to his temple, oddly positioned to look like a gun. "All a state of mind." He sauntered off, straightening his jacket and making room for his crotch as he walked, swinging his feet at the ankles to shake off wrinkles.

"Close your mouth, Tucker. You're gawking," T.J. reminded him.

"That's a complicated man right there," murmured Tucker. "I can see how he gutted out twenty years on the Teams. Thank God Brawley made it. Would hate to be a son of his and not make a Team."

"You know the family better, but I'm guessing being on the Teams was summer camp compared to growing up in the Hanks household."

Tucker knew T.J. was right. They'd grown up together in Oregon, and the two boys got acquainted by competing for spots in high school sports teams. They joined their BUD/S class together, but Tucker disengaged after ten years. Brawley re-upped for a short tour and was going to leave as well. Then he met Dorie, so he extended and used the bonus to buy a house. Dorie had a lot to do with that decision.

The rest of the wedding party began to spill out onto the walkway leading to the sanctuary. Blossoming orange trees gave off a gentle and pleasant aroma. Tucker punched Brawley hard in the bicep, nearly knocking him over before he gave the groom and his groomsmen a fat-fingered wave. He was going to find a seat toward the front, but not too close, give himself enough room to spread out in case he fell asleep during the wedding. His goal was to keep his big mouth shut and his eyes glazed over so he could just swim a little with his former Teammates without getting into trouble. That meant he'd keep his hands to himself and wouldn't ask anyone to dance. He'd also pretend not to look for cleavage or evidence of a proud bony mound or ample ass beneath layers of swirling chiffon and taffeta.

Piece of cake, he thought as he entered the sanctuary. Organ music played, accompanied by a violin and flute combination.

Hospital music.

The two Hanks sisters were dressed in identical maroon dresses with white lace collars, revealing their beanpole stature. Both girls had their long brown hair parted in the middle, tied in a bun at the back of their neck. No curls, ribbons, or sparkles to adorn them.

Each had a deep pink lily wrist corsage on their right hands, folded identically next to each other.

The moms were ushered in next. Mrs. Hanks wore a darker shade of maroon, but her brownish grey hair was pulled back similar to her daughters'. Mr. Hanks looked around the room, catching eyes of friends and landing briefly on Tucker's face. He sat down hard, making the pew squeak.

Dorie's mom was lead in by Riley Branson. The lady was the same kind of bombshell for the older crowd, and Brawley had told Tucker stories of her younger years growing up in San Diego. Though she was close to sixty, her hair was as blonde as her daughter's gorgeous locks. She wore a tailored light pink suit with a flared waist jacket covered in glistening crystals that flashed all over the interior of the narthex and the aisle going down. The skirt below her tiny waist didn't leave much to the imagination. She wasn't as tall as her daughter, so the high heels were giving her some trouble on the cushy rug.

Dorie's mother sat next to her already seated boyfriend, an obvious sign that he might not be a permanent fixture in the family, but he gave her a peck on the cheek anyway.

The organ music crescendo rose, and a majestic non-wedding style march was on, signaling that the audience should rise for the bride and her father.

Everyone came to their feet, Tucker one of the last to stand. He turned to the narthex and saw beautiful Dorie all decked out in bright white. Ahead of her were several bridesmaids, all Barbies, except for one, who was a big girl with about the largest chest Tucker had ever seen. He found himself praying for a clothing malfunction as she paraded down the aisle with Riley. Her tight bustier looked like it was going to explode any second, which might even knock Riley off his feet. He found himself chuckling under his breath at the image in his head until someone in the row ahead of him turned around with a frown.

But Tucker's daydream was shattered by the presence of Dorie, looking every bit the virginal angel. She was probably the prettiest bride he'd ever seen. Her veil was loaded with little crystals, like her mother's suit. By candlelight at the evening service, it created the effect of a thousand little faeries dancing down the aisle all around her. Mr. Carlson looked tanned and about as proud as a father could be, since his daughter was marrying a war hero.

Brawley was gaping and looked pale as the creamy skin on his bride's beautiful face. His best man whispered something to him, which caused a quick glance to his crotch, followed by an annoyed sigh as he realized his best man was messing with him. He presented his elbow to Dorie as her father kissed her good-bye. Dorie grabbed Brawley's hand instead.

Tucker prepped himself so that he wouldn't fall asleep, but found he needed very little help. The girls were ten point fives, even the heavy one. He told himself to stop it several times, but he was used to ranking women in front of him. Dorie would be number one, of course. Then there was that red-head, but the dark-haired heavy one kept catching his eye. He matched them all up to her, and, to his surprise, his dick preferred her.

The Hanks sisters began a duet that was about as bloodless as the middle-aged female lab tech at the VA who actually sported a five o'clock shadow. It was about as pleasant, too. The slightly off-key rendition of a country song he couldn't remember had people in the audience coughing to clear the pain in their ears. Tucker was going to burst out laughing if he wasn't careful. He opened a package of gum, made too much noise, and found people frowning at him.

Who cares? He chomped his gum silently and appeared not to notice.

With that out of the way, he tried to concentrate on the words of the reverend's message to the audience, and that's when he fell asleep. He startled from a very pleasant dream to find several in the crowd reminding him they still didn't approve. An older bony fist leaned over his shoulder to hand him a tissue because he had drooled on himself.

Can I help it? Sermons put me to sleep.

Then he noticed the dark-haired plus sized girl staring right at him with daggers. Okay, so he messed that one up. But he wasn't there to take home a date anyhow, so he shrugged, stopped looking at the girls, and started staring back at the people in the audience who had caught the snoring or grunting or drooling— maybe all three.

I need some spiked punch.

He knew that someone was going to do it. Mrs. Hanks had forbidden alcohol, but she was about to learn a lesson. It was no SEAL wedding if there wasn't a heavy dose of alcohol.

Come on. Come on. Let's get the party going.

The rings were exchanged. The kiss was pornographic, as a good SEAL should behave, and included a gentle squeeze of the bride's ass, which made her giggle when they both got tangled up in her veil. Tucker noticed the big girl didn't like that, either.

Mercifully, the wedding was over. Brawley and his young nymph floated down the aisle, followed by the bevy of lovelies, Tucker was suddenly jealous that T.J. had accompanied the brunette. The shit-eating grin he gave Tucker in exchange meant he knew full well what he was doing as his elbow leaned a little deeper into the lady's chest, which extended her left boob and created about eight inches of mouth-watering cleavage.

I got assholes for friends.

But since T.J. was happily married to the lovely Shannon, Tucker didn't have to worry about anything.

Except to keep from drooling, get drunk with dignity, and pretend this was a good idea.

Because it wasn't. He knew he'd made one of the biggest mistakes of his life.

CHAPTER 2

BRANDY WAS GLAD the party was beginning. Her plan was to get considerably sauced, dousing and putting out the fires of a disastrous year. She'd been let go earlier in the year for speaking a little too plainly to a customer of the advertising firm. A competing agency hired her the next week—until she found out they were moving their operation to Silicon Valley from San Diego. Her father still owned and operated the local organic grocery store, and so Brandy came back to work for him until something else came on the horizon.

When Dorie asked her to be part of the wedding party, her decision to stay in Southern California was set in stone.

Thinking it would be helpful to meet her diet goals for the wedding she took up a part-time job as a weight loss counselor. The free meal plans and extra income were at first a double bonus. She had some early success, but then her diet stalled and crashed. The food started tasting like cardboard, and she was secretly supplementing with things from her dad's store. Her lack of progress and her MIA at weigh-ins caused another termination.

But that was last year. This was New Years Eve, and she was going to have a great year. She'd land that dream job after all, get down to a size eight or ten—one she'd never achieved before—and who knows what else could happen? Perhaps Prince Charming would notice her new svelte physique. She'd start lifting weights and perhaps learn to run so she could enter a 5k with Dorie.

She watched the bride and groom glide over the dance floor. The weather was spectacular and clear, surprisingly warm. By candlelight, they swayed and swooned, and there wasn't a woman in the crowd who didn't want to trade places with Dorie and her handsome new husband. The hush that fell over the group made her begin to cry. The glittery twinkle lights and silky drapes at the sides of the tent blew in the gentle breeze coming right off the bay.

She approached the group of her fellow bridesmaids and noticed their chatter stopped the instant she was upon them. Several brittle smiles greeted her.

"Having a good time, Brandy?" asked one of them.

"Isn't it the most gorgeous wedding you've ever

seen?" she answered, aware she was gushing like a schoolgirl.

"I'm looking at all the eye candy," one of the other girls remarked, nodding to the group of nearly twenty young men, all fit and handsome, dressed in black tuxes and suits.

"Your Randy is deployed, Sheila. You can look, but better not touch."

"I hear that the guys on SEAL Team 5 don't have much to do with these boys. They're all Team 3."

Brandy was disgusted with her attitude, but the rest of the crowd tittered, and closed ranks. Soon she was left alone as they wafted off to grab some punch. On the way, two girls were asked to join the dance floor, as other couples from the partygoers began to pour into the revelry. In a matter of minutes, the bride and groom were hidden by other dancers. When the tune turned lively, the dance floor got even more crowded.

Earlier, she'd watched one of the SEALs on Brawley's team add some rum to the punch, along with something else, so she was fairly sure it would be strong. But just in case, she had a flask of brandy, her namesake and always a good companion in case the evening turned lonely.

She checked her watch as she headed to the punch and saw it was forty-five to midnight, the beginning of the New Year. Soon all those bad dreams of this year would be wiped away forever.

As she reached for a glass, another hand crossed hers. In the collision, several drinks fell to the floor, and several more fell over on themselves on the pretty lace tablecloth, making a light pink stain. The hand she'd collided with could easily palm a basketball or clean off a windshield with one swipe. Enormous beefy fingers, dripping in the sweet mixture, shook, sending droplets of punch all over her face and upper chest. The surprising spritzer caught her off guard.

A deep voice made an apology to the plain woman behind the punchbowl who looked like she'd faint from fear. Then the voice came her way.

"So sorry. I didn't mean to make a mess."

It was the beast from the sanctuary, the one who reminded her of Shrek. And now he even sounded like Shrek. She stared up at massive shoulders and a puffed out chest so large he could have trouble getting through a doorway without going sideways. He wasn't young, like the other men, with a healthy dose of salt and pepper in his hair and a solid white full beard. It was a lot to take in, but she finally found his eyes, and that settled her nerves just a bit.

"Are you okay?" he whispered. His warm eyes twinkled and were kind.

"Y-Y-Yes." Then she felt the coolness of the punch covering her. "Napkin."

It was quickly delivered to her flailing hand.

"Another one. I need another one," she said since the small napkin began to fall apart as she dabbed her face.

He handed her a fistful nearly an inch thick.

"Oh! That's too many," she mumbled, but took the wad anyway.

"You got a lot on your-your-your chest there. I hope it doesn't stain." He pulled her aside to make way for one of the caterers to mop up the floor.

The slip made her angry. He gave her a fistful of napkins because of the *size* of her chest. She turned her back to him and continued to dab off the droplets dripping down between her breasts. Out of the corner of her eye she saw one of the other bridesmaids whisper to her neighbor.

She abruptly turned again so she could address the monster, but the area was vacant. She caught sight of his back and head as he ducked under the tent cover and walked out into the night.

The young catering staff member brought her a filled cup of punch. "Here you go. Don't be concerned about this. That guy looks like an accident waiting to happen. Not your fault."

"Thanks." It was all she could think of to say.

The punch was indeed strong, and Brandy discovered upon finishing it that, although she was relaxed, her breathing was still just as difficult. She tried not to think about the help she'd needed getting the big undergarment on before the bustier could go on. It took two of the bridesmaids to work alternating to get the large zipper to close. At one point, she thought her breasts would reach her chin, but she was able to position herself until she was somewhat comfortable. The bustier was easier, since it closed with a row of large hooks and eyes.

She wobbled her way to the women's restroom and reapplied lipstick, really laying it on heavy. She loved the bright red shade of her new purchase. Adding a little blush, removing two dried droplets of punch, and rinsing her dress with a little water, she felt put together and ready to take on the world. It was only twenty minutes to midnight. All this would go into the folder of old news in just a little while.

Brawley was standing at the edge of the dance floor, watching his friends taking turns dancing with his bride.

"She's lovely, Brawley. I'm surprised you share her," she said and smiled.

The handsome SEAL had always been nice to her. Her crush on him was hard to hide. He leaned over and whispered in her ear, "Well then, let's make her jealous. You game?"

When he leaned back to check her expression, she

gave him the biggest smile she could muster.

"Game on, mister."

They danced a modified swing to a lively Motown classic. She knew Brawley had benefitted from the instructions he had taken with Dorie. Brandy had taken lessons with her father after her mother passed. The two of them moved around the floor like a choreographed routine, causing a clapping circle to be formed around them. Brawley's bow tie was undone, as were the top two buttons on his shirt. Brandy wished she could remove or disconnect something, too, but in the end, she stopped just long enough to take off her shoes and throw them into the corner. Brawley swung her around with his powerful arms. She felt lighter than air.

This is a good way to usher in the new year.

Finally the music ended and the crowd cheered them. Brawley gave her a big bear hug that nearly toppled them both. She regained her balance, and, breathing heavy, she accepted his polite kiss to her cheek—a cheek she would hate to wash off.

Dorie was smiling as she re-attached herself to her beau, using his handkerchief to wipe the sweat from his forehead. All Brandy could do was watch them.

The room seemed to rumble behind her, but it was only the sound of the beast's voice.

"Tell you what. I'll go kidnap Dorie, and then you

can have him."

Even the hair at the back of her neck stood straight out. Her shoulders felt the tiny beads of moist breath against her flesh. It set up a vibration that traveled briefly down her spine. It was a curious reaction, especially for someone so beast-like.

Upon turning, she faced his warm brown eyes again. They were still twinkling little laugh lines evident at the sides. Somewhere the bevy of brides-maids and their friends were laughing, and she didn't care.

"That would never work. Brawley would be too heartbroken. He'd probably throw himself off the Coronado Bridge." Her tongue nearly stuck to the roof of her mouth. "I need something to drink."

"I think we should try this punch thing again, don't you?" His voice was gentle, almost melodic, but very, very deep. She felt the words vibrate in her chest.

"Yes, let's try to do it better this time. I think they're out of napkins," she answered.

Was that a growl she heard? She wasn't sure. But it was a wicked growl that could fend off anything.

They walked together side by side.

"I'm Tucker," he said flatly.

"And I'm Brandy."

At the table, he chose the larger clear plastic cups, handing her one and taking the other for himself.

"To a new year. No accidents," he said.

She met his cup with a dull click. "No accidents. To a perfect year."

The cool drink was refreshing, and she finished the whole glass faster than he did. His face was full of surprise.

"All that dancing," she said between deep breaths, "I needed that. Probably should have had water—"

All of a sudden, she felt light-headed. The air constriction had finally caught up with the alcohol floating around her stomach and brain. As she began to see black spots in front of her eyes, she felt his arm underneath her back, holding her, keeping her from falling. Just before she blacked out, she heard the words,

"I've got you. No worries."

CHAPTER 3

TUCKER CARRIED HER to a row of chairs setting just outside the tent. He hurried to get her out before they attracted much attention. Instinctively, he knew she'd be embarrassed if she caused another incident.

She was beginning to moan as he did a light jog towards the chairs. He laid her down, then removed his coat and placed it over her, pulling it up all the way to under her chin.

"Brandy, stay right here and stay warm. I'm going to get some water and a clean washcloth for your forehead. But stay here, okay?"

He saw her nod. Her face was pale, and she'd attempted to open her eyes, but closed them again with another moan. He suspected she'd be sick next.

He ran to the curtains where the catering equipment and staff were housed and got a clean dishcloth and a bottle of sparkling water. When he returned to Brandy, she had already rolled over on her side and was starting to vomit.

"It's okay. You eat anything today?"

She shook her head and then retched nothing but a pink liquid. All she had on her stomach was alcohol.

"You need to eat something. That will soak up some of the alcohol."

She ignored him and retched again. He held her hair back from her face before wiping her forehead, cheeks, and then finally cleaned her lips. He helped her roll back.

"Not too far back. Stay on your side. It might help."

She sighed and snuggled under his jacket. "I hope I didn't get your tux."

"Nope. All's safe. You were actually quite dainty about it. You should see it when I get sick. Not a pretty sight."

"I can only imagine," she mumbled. Then her hand searched and grabbed his as she opened her eyes. "Sorry. Sorry. I'm so sorry. I didn't mean that."

"Yes, you did." He held her hand, and then his thumb began to rub over her knuckles. He stopped himself. "You didn't eat anything before you drank. It happens to the best of us. I'm going to get you something."

"No. I'm on a diet."

"Hogwash," he said as he got up and headed for the food tables. Glancing back, he saw that her gaze followed him. He loosened his tie and unbuttoned his collar. Brawley was on him with concern written all over his face.

"Is she okay?"

"She's gonna be fine. Liquor on an empty stomach. She just needed some fresh air, and I'm getting her something to eat." He searched the small finger sandwiches and bypassed the frittata and vegetables.

"You let me know, promise?" Brawley answered. "We're cutting the cake at midnight. Just a couple of minutes now."

"I'm on medic duty, but I can only imagine what that kiss is gonna look like. You gonna mess up her face with it?"

"Nah. I wanna get laid tonight, Tucker. It's my wedding night."

"Smart move. Don't worry about Brandy."

"She's in good hands." Brawley winked and left to join the crowd gathered around the cake.

Tucker piled the dish with the sandwiches and returned to Brandy. She was attempting to sit up. He knelt in front of her. "I've got some bread here, which should be good for your stomach. Some kind of mystery meat in the middle, so go easy."

She had pulled his jacket around her shoulders. She smiled. Her beautiful chest and cleavage was hard not to stare at, so he focused on the plate offered to her.

She popped the little sandwich into her mouth and closed her eyes.

"Hits the spot."

"Good." He took one. "They're not bad. You should have another."

Brandy did as she was instructed.

"Feeling any better?"

She nodded. Her hair was hanging down over her shoulders as she put her elbows and forearms on her thighs. The gap in her bustier was enormous.

"I wish I could take this damned thing off and go topless."

"A dangerous thought," he said, slightly embarrassed she'd caught him looking.

She smiled. "So tell me something, Tucker. Did someone put you up to this? Be nice to the fat girl?"

The thought had never occurred to him. He was surprised.

"No. No one put me up to anything. Why, you think there's something unattractive about you? Are you an axe murderer or serial killer or something I should be afraid of?"

She shrugged and gave a small laugh. "You know the expression. Age old tale. *Always a bridesmaid, never a bride.* That sort of thing."

"Whoa!" Tucker handed her the plate and stood up. "Who said anything about being a bride. If you're thinking—"

"Happy New Year," came the shout from the tent.

He looked down at her. She'd set the sandwiches to the side, took a deep breath, and said, "Shut up and kiss me, you idiot."

With the room erupting in horn and popper noises, Tucker came back to his knees, reached for her face, and melted his lips into hers. It wasn't the wedding cake kiss Brawley would have, and tasted like a ham sandwich, but it definitely got the sparks going deep inside him. Almost painfully, his libido lumbered into full action mode. He felt like a battleship heading out to sea on its final mission. His heart pounded, almost hurting from inattention and need. The subtle scent from her perfume and the way her hair felt on his cheek nearly made him dizzy.

He pulled back and looked into her eyes.

"You okay?" he asked.

"I'd be better if you kissed me again. I needed that."

Her fingers sifted through his hair. Their deep kiss left them both breathless. As his cheek set against hers, he whispered, "What was that?"

"You okay?" she asked, twisting the conversation and letting her eyes flirt. Her forefinger traced over his lips as she focused on them. He squeezed her shoulders but kept his hands in place. He desperately wanted to explore what was being so cruelly smashed underneath all that fabric.

He'd promised himself he wouldn't be looking tonight and would keep his hands to himself. But his promise was going down in flames. He just wasn't sure what he should do. He knew what he desired, but he didn't want to take advantage of her, since he was fairly sure she was still pretty drunk.

"I don't do this," he finally said.

"I don't, either."

"I mean—what I meant was, you're drunk, and I don't think it's right to—"

"If you've changed your mind, just say so. Don't blame it on honor or some other BS, Tucker. I'm a big girl. I can smell a turn down when it's coming. I'm used to it."

His heart was breaking for whatever her experiences had been in the past. It was clear there was some damage there. But it just didn't add up. He could not see any reason she should feel that way.

She'd started to stand, began to remove his jacket.

"Wait, Brandy. You got it all wrong."

"It's okay. Don't patronize me."

"Damnit. I'm not patronizing you. Would you get that goddamned chip off your fuckin' shoulder, Brandy? What I'm telling you is I'm attracted to you. And I don't want to take advantage. I'm not that kind of guy."

He stood with her, putting the jacket back around her shoulders.

"Cake?" A silver tray with slices of wedding cake was presented to them by one of the wait staff.

Brandy eyed the tray, and Tucker could tell she wanted a piece. He took two plates. She was weaving slightly, so he guided her to sit back down. Then he got on his knees again, setting one plate aside. He cut a piece without frosting and held it in front of her. "Probably not the best thing for you to eat, but it might not be that bad."

She watched him while she opened her mouth. He placed the cake on her tongue.

"Perfect. Delicious. More. With frosting," she said.

"Brandy, you sure?" He could see some of the earlier dreaminess return to her eyes.

"What if I put some frosting here," she said as she touched the top of her cleavage with her forefinger. "Or what if it got smeared lower. Would you lick it off?"

Tucker's knees were shaking as his groin refused to behave. He inhaled her scent and the way her eyes were half-lidded while she dipped her finger in the frosting and slowly slid it down between her breasts. She leaned back on the chair, spread her knees, and dared him with her eyes.

His mouth watered as his tongue tasted her flesh

beneath the sweet fluffy frosting. He sucked, pulling the top of her right breast into his mouth just short of creating a mark. But he wanted to. He wanted to see her naked, her nipples dripping with frosting, her sex wet with her desire for him. He needed to lose himself in those breasts as he took her deep.

Her fingertips touched his temples. She kissed his forehead, holding his head to her chest. Then one hand slid down the outside of his shirt to his waistband.

"Can I take you home with me?" she breathed into his ear.

"Darlin', I'll go with you anywhere. You just name it."

"I should go get my shoes."

"I'll get them. But I don't think you'll need them."

"Why?"

"Because, sweetheart, I'm going to carry you."

"Really? Why?"

"Because it's just what's done on New Years. You stay right here, and I'll go get them. You think about having that perfect year. You think about what a perfect night would be like, and then let's go do it. Okay?"

He could feel her eyes on his back as he made his return to the party. One of the bridesmaids tried to drag him to the dance floor. She got his shirttails untucked from his waistband before he got away. In the corner were Brandy's heels. He dipped to pick them up and sauntered right through the center of the dance floor, carrying his trophy in his right hand.

He saw the looks. He saw the surprise. He saw Mr. Hanks nod and smile some secret appreciation. Dorie winked at him. Brawley gave him a thumbs up.

He was back. Tucker was back in the real world. The night had turned from the biggest mistake of his life to something else quite extraordinary.

It was going to be the best night of his life. And this was only the start of a new year.

CHAPTER 4

B RANDY SAT BACK in Tucker's bright red truck that set so high she doubted she'd be able to mount it without help. But Tucker had placed her delicately on the seat, strapping her in securely, and then pressing a warm-up kiss to her willing lips. In his own way, he was gentle, but it took effort to not break or hurt things, she noted. The engine revved, and then the truck lurched, headed to Brandy's cottage. She decided not to tell him her father lived in the house in front.

The inside of the cab smelled like him. He fiddled and adjusted the heater, asking if she was comfortable. It was only a ten-minute ride, but in that short time, she noted how he and the huge truck were one giant machine, like a Transformer. The dash and black leather seats were immaculately polished. The floor mats washed like a brand new vehicle. She noted a little decal on the driver's side of the windshield, shaped like an anchor.

When they arrived at her cottage, she was grateful all the lights were out at her father's house. Tucker insisted on carrying her to the front door and then let her slide down the front of him. There were bulging body parts she rubbed against, which would be impossible to miss.

She fumbled for her keys and then led him inside.

Tucker made her small living room feel even smaller. The cottage was a converted outbuilding. Therefore, the ceilings were a few inches lower than normal. He ducked and followed her to the single bedroom. Along the way, she asked, "You want anything to drink?"

His eyes were fixated on her. The slow shake of his head was sexy and deliberate. "No ma'am."

"I'm going to need some help getting out of this."

"Just show me what to do."

"There are these hooks at the back," she said as she turned to show him. "You have to undo them one at a time."

Tucker fumbled with the fabric and the closures. She could tell he was getting frustrated. "Holy cow, Brandy. How in the devil would you get yourself out of this thing by yourself?"

"I can pull it over my head, but it would be easier if—"

At last several of the hooks were released, and she was grateful for the extra breathing space.

"You got it."

The bustier fell to the ground. Brandy unzipped her skirt and laid it over a chair. The ugly diaphragm-squeezing undergarment was the only thing between them. She removed her stockings and panties, and once again presented her back to him.

"This is going to be hard. You have to unzip me here."

Tucker was on it, his huge fingers slipping beneath the off-white fabric, while his other hand grabbed the zipper and had it undone in just a couple of seconds.

"Piece of cake."

The rush of air to her lungs was so sudden she nearly fainted again. He braced her before she could fall over. He pulled her to his chest while his hands took hold of her ass and squeezed until it hurt.

She began to unbutton his shirt, then lifted the cotton tee shirt up, and kissed him, placing her palms over his pecs. She reached below, fingers creeping into his pants when he quickly undid his belt and stepped out of them.

She was going to step to press herself against him, but he abruptly picked her up and brought her over to the bed, where he gently placed her down.

"You have some protection?" he whispered as he kissed her neck. One callused hand squeezed her left breast and then slid down lower.

She started to sit up to grab the condoms from the bedside table, but he pressed her back, rising to his knees and staring down at her.

His hands massaged both boobs now. "You're incredible. I think I've died and gone to Heaven," he said as he nuzzled her cleavage, sucking and pinching her nipples. His scratchy beard tickled as his kissing moved lower until he was at her core. His thumbs pressed her open, rubbing her nub as she shuddered with anticipation.

She watched him pleasure her, his giant shoulders rising and falling as he dipped lower. He kept one hand massaging her breast. He was nearly delicate the way he explored with his fingers and tongue. It filled her with electricity as she heard him moan between her legs. She pulled his hair, massaged his temples, and then writhed to the feel of his fingers inside her, calling her to ride his hand and lose herself for him. She came up to her knees, reaching for his cock while she pressed herself into his giant palm.

She gripped him, moving up and down, squeezing his balls and covering his tip with precum. After some minutes of play, she raised herself up and reached for the drawer, bringing out the condom, then tearing it open with her teeth. As she looked up to him in the moonlight, their mouths closed on each other, tongues exploring, becoming more and more intense. Her fingers slid the thin condom down his shaft and massaged him while they finished their slow, sensuous kiss.

Tucker leaned back and brought her up on top of him. With her knees hugging his hips, he gripped her body, snagging her sex on his cock and then pressing her down so he was deep inside her.

He was urgent to move against her, raising and lowering her on him, drawing the rhythm faster and faster until he quickly picked her up, threw her back against the mattress, and mounted her. Plunging deep, he buried his head in her chest.

They moved together like old dance partners, reveling in the miracle that was their bodies. Beneath him, she felt delicate. She melted under his kiss, rising again into multiple orgasms as he plundered and then softened his penetration.

He was an innovative lover, consumed with desire for her, yet very attentive to her needs, begging her to come and then thanking her as she shattered beneath him over and over again. She knew that as the minutes turned into the early pre-dawn hours of the morning, she had never before felt so loved, so coveted and consumed. As the first rays of early dawn shone through the window, he held her close as he came hard and deep inside her, then folded her into his arms, and fell asleep.

She worried her beating heart would wake him as she luxuriated in the heat between them. Every cell in her body screamed for him. Her ear was pressed against his chest, and she listened as air filled his lungs and then expelled. Her skin was bathed in the sweet sweat between their bodies, the way her legs wrapped around his enormous thighs, and how his arms squeezed her so tight it rivaled the bustier just before she fell asleep.

But in the shelter of his arms, there was room to breathe, and finally to dream about a perfect evening, and the beginning of a perfect year.

CHAPTER 5

A SLIVER OF bright sunlight traveled slowly across Tucker's face like a laser. At first, he startled, since his own apartment was heavily draped in blackout shades. Even on workdays, he was able to sleep in until at least eight. This seemed just minutes from when he'd last closed his eyes.

And then he felt her moist flesh melting all over him. He carefully opened one eye to peer at the lovely brunette resting on his chest. Her lips were still puckered and red, her cheek bulging against her nose. *And she drooled!*

He tilted his head back to avoid giving a belly laugh that would surely wake her. He didn't want to be robbed of these delicious moments. How could he have met a girl who drooled in her sleep?

He scanned the walls of her bedroom. She had tacked several tissue paper sketches of what looked like produce labels and several other ones of large flowers done in chalk or pencil. There was a sketch of a light pink sandy beach cradling white surf coming from a bright turquoise ocean. He noticed a poster made from a picture of Brandy dressed in a large purple grape costume. She was holding a bottle of wine and standing next to Dorie, in an identical costume. Their legs were bright purple from the knees down as they stood in a large stainless steel vat, stomping grapes.

She had a calendar with pictures of beaches from around the world and a photo of her as a young girl sitting beside an older gentleman driving a tractor at a pumpkin farm. Her burgundy bustier and bridesmaid skirt were draped over an easy chair, mixed with his black pants, white shirt, and red white and blue cotton boxers. He was a little embarrassed at the rah rah in his underwear, but he couldn't help it. It was the way he was.

Her bookshelf burst with paperbacks, spilling over onto the floor in several stacks. It appeared every one of them had a picture of a naked man on the cover. The bedside table still gaped with the open drawer containing a box of condoms. He noticed she owned a bright pink vibrator, and that nearly ruined his composure.

But it was all good. All normal. These were the trappings of a woman he'd been trained to protect. Her precious way of life was valuable, something worth saving. This was evidence that what he'd done as an elite warrior was all worth it. He hoped to God she never had to endure some of the things he'd seen out there on the other side of the planet, where children inhaled a steady diet of uncertainty, misery, and smoke from the ashes of their crumbling civilization that knew nothing but war. His job was to make sure that war stayed there and didn't come home.

Brandy was moving against him, stroking him like she'd done so delicately last night. Her pubic bone pressed into his thigh. He raised his knee to help intensify the feeling.

At last, she placed her chin on his sternum and fed from his eyes. What did she see? He hoped she wasn't disappointed. He wasn't. He remembered every kiss, every stroke, every shudder, and every time he pinned her to the bed with her arms outstretched, as if he could will himself to climb inside her and shelter in place.

She was twirling his frosty chest hairs, biting her lip, and waiting to say something, or waiting for him to speak first. But he didn't feel under any pressure to talk so he just watched this dark angel with the red lips he was ravenous for. He wanted to see her enormous breasts bounce in the morning sun as she writhed above him. He wanted to see her face as he filled her, made her come.

She opened her mouth to say something when the door to her living room opened and a man's voice called out, "Brinny?"

Brandy scrambled to sit up, taking the sheet with her, which left Tucker completely exposed. If the man in the next room came to the doorway, he'd also notice the enormous hard-on Tucker had developed.

She smirked, whispering, "My father."

He sprung to action and quickly slipped on his patriotic boxers, but remained seated on the bed.

"Just a minute dad. I've got someone here," she shouted to the next room. Twisting the sheet around her, she stepped to the doorway. Tucker got a nice view of her shapely rear, her long mahogany hair falling everywhere about her shoulders and upper back. He'd kissed every vertebra last night, kneaded the cheeks of her ass until she squealed. She could take everything he could give out, and then some. He hated having to be careful in his sex play. Brandy played at the same intensity.

"Oh, fine. Look, I'm headed off to the store. You coming in today?"

"Maybe later this afternoon. Would that work?"

"Sure. Sorry I didn't let you know yesterday, but I'm going to be one short today. If you can, that would really help me out."

"No problem, Dad. How about one or two

o'clock?"

"Great. Hey, how was the wedding?"

She adjusted her sheet again, briefly shooting him a gaze as Tucker lay back on the pillow, his hands clasped behind his head. "Dorie was gorgeous. You should have come. They had a great band, lots of people you knew were there."

"A friend of Brawley's?" her dad whispered, but Tucker could hear it clearly.

Brandy nodded. "Dad, I've gotta go."

"No problem. See you later on this afternoon."

The door closed behind him.

Tucker watched her face recovering from the blush that also sent pink blotches to her upper chest. "That was awkward," she mumbled, fiddling with her fingers and refusing to look back at him.

He was charmed with the blush, but even more interested in getting the sheet off her. "Come here," he whispered.

Her face pinked up again, and he chuckled.

"After all the things we did last night, you expect me to believe you're really shy?"

She began twirling her hair around her forefinger, still avoiding eye contact.

"Come here, Brandy. Just for a little bit. Then I'd like to take you out to breakfast. I'm thinking pancakes."

Her large brown eyes snapped to attention. She crawled on all fours toward him. By the time she reached him, the sheet had been left behind. Her breasts overflowed in his hands as her young body undulated over his groin, pressing against the ridge of his hardness. Her fingers deftly slid his boxers down over his thighs while she guided him to her core. He held the sides of her hips, raised her up, and then plunged her back down on him.

Then he remembered. They'd forgotten the condom. Again. With his fingers digging into her flesh, he stopped her movements completely, knowing he had to ask the question and leave it up to her.

"Is it okay?"

"It's perfect," she blew back at his face, and then she kissed him.

THE SAMOAN PANCAKE House was always a Team favorite on weekends. But today was a holiday so the place was packed. He nodded to several former Teammates, a couple of whom were at the wedding last night.

She chose a corner at the back of the restaurant, and ordered.

"So you used to serve with Brawley, right?"

"About ten years ago. We grew up together in Oregon."

"You're from Oregon?"

He noticed she had a dimple to the right of her mouth, which was cuter than all heck.

"*What?*"

"You have a very sexy dimple right there." He touched the spot and loved her blush, as she held his hand.

"I love it up there. My parents had plans to retire near McMinville, but my mom passed before they could sell everything and go do it. Now Dad's stuck with the store."

"That's close to where Brawley and I grew up."

"That's what I thought. So your family was farmers, then?"

"Still are. My sister and her husband and kids live with them and they all work in the family business."

"Sounds nice. What do they grow?"

Tucker was hesitant to explain the details of his parent's venture, so he deflected the question by giving a half-answer. "They do hydroponics, greenhouse stuff. They used to grow wheat, but over the years, they've sold off parcels so now they only have a few acres left. It's all they can handle."

"You miss Oregon?" Brandy asked as their breakfast was served.

Tucker poured syrup all over his pancakes and even his eggs and the extra biscuit he ordered. "I worked up a regular appetite, Miss Brandy." He winked at her, amused by the way her jaw dropped as she watched him take his first bite. Then she blushed again.

"I don't miss Oregon at all. I like it here. More sun, less rain. More to do outside, and I don't have to prepare for monsoons to do them, either. San Diego suits me just fine."

"Yup," she agreed.

"You grew up here, then?" He knew she had, but wanted to keep the conversation going.

"Right here. I'm not sure if I stay because of Dad or he stays because of me. I work for him, help him out a bit, since I'm between jobs at the moment."

"I thought you worked with Dorie at the ad agency."

"*Used* to. I guess I pissed off a customer. I don't think the advertising business is for me."

"Brawley said your dad's store is quite upscale? Can he make it with Amazon and all those other players fighting for the retail dollar?"

"I think he makes just enough to live on. Dad's not someone who could ever work for anyone else. He owns the market outright, and the half-acre lot behind. He has some fantasy of doing a little truck farming, perhaps grow his own organic produce."

"Farming, even on a half-acre, is a lot of work."

"I think that's the point, Tucker. When he gets tired of it, then he'll sell. This gives him something to do. Keeps him from missing my mother. She was everything to him." Then she added, "I don't think our family does well with retirement. It's kind of a dirty word."

Tucker nodded and completely agreed. "Smart man. Men have to do things. They can't just sit around and watch the world go by. They have to get into action, or at least the men I hang with do."

"So now that you're off the Teams, what do you do?"

"I run some trainings for guys, mostly high school age, who are interested in joining the SEALs. I try to get them in good physical shape to help them pass BUD/S. I'm kind of the guy who tells them the truth, dispels the garbage the recruiters fill them with. I make sure they know what they're signing up for."

"They're lucky to have you."

"It's only part-time, but it gives me a chance to give a little back to the community. I also do some personal training and I work at the glider port, instructing for the skydiving school."

"Skydiving? Wow."

"You should try it sometime. You'd have a ball."

He was surprised to see she appeared resistant.

"No, thanks. I'll stick to the ground, thank you. If

God had wanted me to fly through the air, he would have given me wings."

"Or an expert tandem buddy. It will change your life, Brandy."

"Or end it."

"No. These guys are safe. They train all the SEALs down here. Some of the most experienced skydivers and stuntmen in the country. It's all completely safe." He drew her hand to his mouth and kissed it. "All about trust, Brandy. And finding out about your limits."

They finished breakfast, and Tucker reluctantly took her back to her car. She turned towards him before she got out of the truck.

"I had a great time, Tucker. I had a goal to have one perfect evening, and it was all that and more. Sorry I got sick on you."

He leaned over and cradled her jaw with his palm before kissing her. "I did, too. I don't want to tell you my goal because you dashed it all to hell. This is the part where I ask you if I can see you again. I'm hoping the answer is yes."

She held his hand between both of hers. When she looked up, he thought at first she might say no.

"I was just looking for one perfect night. I guess I could handle two."

CHAPTER 6

BRANDY CHANGED HER clothes and put on her comfortable cross trainers since she'd be standing the entire afternoon. She drove down the strand past the SEAL Qualification course and thought about what it had been like for Tucker and Brawley going through the training together. Many times, she'd watched the boat crews of new recruits working their way over the rocks or running down the beach carrying telephone poles over their heads. She mused that Tucker could actually make a telephone pole look small.

She turned off the highway and into the tree-lined streets of an older suburban neighborhood then headed away from the bay where things were a little more spread out. Small ranchettes dotted the landscape. She came upon the boutique strip mall containing a cluster of specialty stores with her father's organic grocery and deli at one end. She could see his silver pickup truck parked at the side, as well as Kip's beat-up VW. The five time college freshman had worked for her dad ever since he'd mastered the art of riding a bike. He was practically family. There were only a couple of other cars in the lot, indicating they were having a very slow day.

She loved the smell of the produce and the bright colors of the vegetables and fruit every time she arrived. It was like the smell of flowers at a florist. Her dad was famous for carrying unusual fruits from all over the world, but he specialized in California and Florida citrus and always did a huge business every Christmas sending fruit baskets to customer's relatives all over the globe.

She ducked under the portable canvas awnings shading the lovely displays, piled up in pine boxes. Two shoppers wandered down aisles inside the building itself. One was headed in the direction of the checkout, having spotted Brandy arrive.

"I'll be right back," she told the woman. "Just got to grab my apron and punch in."

Inside the store's tiny office was her father's desk, covered in catalogs, papers, and envelopes—most of them unopened. It was obvious he needed help with his bookkeeping and office organization. She intended to have a discussion with him about that very thing, and soon.

Brandy placed her purse inside the top file cabinet

drawer, noticing it had been pushed aside and was slightly crooked. With a couple of shoves she righted it to stand snug against the desk, where it belonged. Her dad's chair was pulled out, and his glasses were folded on top of the closed laptop that was so old the Apple store refused to work on it any longer.

Slipping the kelly-green apron over her head, she deposited her cell phone in the large center pocket, tied the straps behind her waist, and began to look for her father.

"Dad?"

There was no answer so she figured he might be in the large cooler room at the rear.

That's where she found him. He was sprawled on the floor, his face turned to one side. A trickle of blood had seeped into the floorboards coming from under his upper body somewhere. His face was pale, lips slightly purple. She was immediately worried he might be dead.

"Oh my God. Dad! What's happened?"

She fell to her knees and tried to revive him, but his body remained limp. Then she checked for a pulse and was relieved to have found one. And he appeared to be breathing, but when she tried to arouse him again, he didn't respond. His face was cold and clammy.

With her own pulse racing, she dialed 911 and gave instructions to the paramedics who promised they'd be there within minutes.

She called out for Kip, but again received no answer.

"Hang in there, dad."

But her father didn't register any response, which sent a spear of panic down her spine. She wasn't sure if she should roll him over on his back and decided it would be safer to just leave him on his side. Beneath his head she felt the sticky dark red blood. Finding a clean hand towel, she applied slight pressure, hoping to stop the bleeding. In mere seconds, the towel was bright red and soaked. Her hands were dripping in her father's blood. She carefully rested his head against the soaked cotton and staggered out front to see if she could find Kip. It was hard to concentrate, but she managed to calm her nerves.

The customer was waiting not-so-patiently by the checkout, but when she spied Brandy's bloody hands, she began to scream. Brandy jumped as if she'd been slapped.

"Hold on. My father has taken a spill, and the paramedics are on their way. Give me a minute to get myself gathered. Have you seen Kip?"

The woman closed her mouth and merely shook her head briskly. "Who's Kip?"

"He's the other clerk here."

"I didn't see anyone."

Brandy looked at the woman's basket, then at the

counter and discovered the cash register drawer had been pried open and was completely empty. A check was crumpled at her feet. It began to dawn on her that perhaps this had been a robbery attempt gone badly.

"Ma'am, it looks like we've been robbed, too. You sure you didn't see anyone?"

"No. No one was here. These folks," she said, pointing to a couple behind her, "arrived after me. Is your dad okay?"

"No. I'm worried. He's unconscious, but help is on the way."

Just then, she heard the familiar sound of Kip parking the company van. He entered the store, tossing and catching his keys. Upon seeing Brandy, he gave her a big grin. "Hey there."

"Kip, Dad's fallen. He's in the back. I've called the paramedics and they're on their way. This woman wants to check out, but I need to stand guard with Dad until the paramedics come. Can you get the backup working? If not, can we just close down the store?"

"Sure thing." Kip was already on his knees, extracting another register from under the counter, connecting the telephone feeds, and adjusting the paper. "I've got this. You go be with your dad."

She jogged to the back of the storeroom. Her father still hadn't moved.

She was relieved to hear the sirens getting closer

until she saw just flashing red lights. Someone must have directed them to the rear because two paramedics ran through the back door and bent over to attend to her father. Their fingers deftly poked and repositioned his head and neck, checking out his neck, arms, and legs.

"Did you see him fall?" the handsome dark-uniformed rescue worker asked her as he scanned her bloody hands. He turned his attention back to her father, focusing on the bleeding from his head.

"No. I got here like ten or fifteen minutes ago. I expected to find him in the store, so I went looking for him and found him here. Just like this. I put the towel under his head. But there was so much...blood." Her voice wavered.

The other paramedic was up on her feet, barking instructions into the com strapped to her shoulder.

"Are you a relative or co-worker?" the male paramedic asked.

"I'm his daughter."

"What's his name?"

"Steven Cook."

"He have any illnesses or things I need to know? Medications?"

"Geez." Brandy wracked her brain, trying to remember if he'd told her anything about his health, and came up blank. "I don't think he takes anything. As far as illnesses, not that he's told me."

"How old is he?"

"Sixty-two."

"No pacemakers, history of stroke or heart attack?"

"No. Not that I know of. I really don't know. He's been healthy."

"So you didn't see how this happened?"

"No."

"Anybody angry with him for some reason?"

"No, why?"

"Sorry to have to tell you, but this was no accidental fall. It appears he was hit at the back of the head, you see here?"

He showed her a dark mass of clotted blood, hair, and tissue at the back of his head, slightly underneath him.

"And then it appears he fell, because this other wound looks like it happened when his head hit the floor. So we got two head injuries to deal with."

"I see." Brandy tried to sound as calm as the paramedic was. But in spite of her efforts, her teeth began to chatter.

"You going to be okay?" he asked.

"I don't like blood," she whispered. Black dots began obscuring her vision, and she could tell she was close to passing out.

The paramedic's quick thinking had him grabbing

her upper arms with his bloody gloved hands and positioning her on a nearby chair. "Put your head between your knees if you need to. I'll get you some water in a minute. Better?"

She was starting to get confused and could feel her breathing becoming labored. So much was happening.

"Breathe. Take deep breaths," he commanded.

Her father still wasn't moving. His dark lips were getting darker by the minute. She abruptly threw off his hands. "Dad. He looks terrible! He's worse!"

"We got it. Just don't want you to die on me, okay?"

The woman paramedic returned with a gurney, which she lowered and positioned next to her father. She cut his long-sleeved shirt with scissors and then started an IV before helping her partner lift him onto the bed. They raised the legs on the cart, clicked it into position, and ran toward the back of the van. The woman stayed behind while the male worker came back to check on Brandy.

"Where can I get you some water? This *is* a store, right?" he asked.

"There's a case on the other side of this wall. Take a couple for yourselves, too."

He was back in seconds, snapping open the plastic cap and holding the bottle up to her mouth.

Brandy guzzled the cool liquid, trying to keep up,

but wound up spilling much of it down her front. She didn't care.

"That help some?"

"I'll be fine."

"You have someone you can call?"

"Kip's here. I want to go be with my dad at the hospital."

"No, not in your condition. But we're taking him to Scripps. You can meet us there. No way I want you driving by yourself."

"Gene?" his partner inserted herself in the exit. "We gotta go now."

"Okay, we're outta here. The police will be arriving soon, so you'll have to give them a statement. Then get someone to bring you down. Right now, we gotta focus on Mr. Cook. So, you take care."

"Thank you so much." She started to stand, but he pushed her shoulders down.

"Don't be stubborn. Be smart."

She didn't like the comment, but she didn't have the energy to fight him back with some quick witty thing. If he only knew.

Stubborn is my middle name.

THE POLICE INTERVIEWED them both, promising to be brief so she could get to the hospital to see her father.

Kip answered another question. "He asked me to

do the home deliveries because he knew you were coming in." He spoke directly to her.

"How long were you gone?" the officer persisted.

"Hour? Maybe an hour and a half. Normally, I'd go later, but I asked to get off early." He turned to Brandy again. "I got a date."

That's when she realized so did she. She'd promised to meet Tucker at the Rusty Scupper after work. He was working at the skydiving school all afternoon.

"You know of anyone who would want to hurt Mr. Cook?" the officer asked.

Brandy shook her head from side to side. "He doesn't have any fights or enemies of any kind. Everyone loves him."

"Well," Kip interrupted, "there is this one thing. He had a guy he let go last week. Several customers complained about him. Too friendly with the younger girls. I'm talking thirteen, fourteen-year-olds."

"When did this happen?" the officer asked.

"Thursday, I think. Jorge Mendoza. I never liked him. Steve got him from some church group recommendation. He'd been staying at a halfway house. I told your dad he was stealing beer and drinking on his breaks, but he didn't care until he started getting the complaints. Tats, even on his face. He stared at people. Cold eyes. Not a good dude at all. I was glad Steve let him go."

"I didn't know about any of that." Brandy admitted it was just like her dad to give someone a chance.

Several customers came asking questions, after hearing the sirens and seeing the police activity. Brandy told them they were closing for the day, and that her father was in the hospital. The police reminded her afterwards not to give out many details.

"Your father keep records here? Any way we could get this guy's address?"

"Um, yes. He keeps his records in the office, but I'll have to dig a bit. He's not the most organized owner out there. Some of it, he keeps in the safe," Brandy answered. One of the officers followed her, and she was able to get the employee folder from the second file drawer. She lifted a heavy canvas seed sack to access her father's safe and found it gaping open. "Holy crap."

Kip was at the doorway in a flash. "Ah shit. I was afraid of that." He put his hand over his mouth. "Sorry, Brandy."

"Did everyone who worked here know about the safe?" one officer asked.

"I wouldn't think so, but then, Dad was pretty trusting." shrugged Brandy.

Kip added, "We were really busy over the weekend with New Years coming up. Everyone was shopping for last minute things. I think he closed early last night. I'm sure he didn't make it to the bank. It's a shame, but

I'm guessing he had a lot of cash in that vault."

"Which points to Mendoza again," said one of the officers.

Brandy took another long gulp of her water, finishing it off. Her eyes filled with tears. Her day had gone from spectacular to tragic. She needed to go be at her father's side. And what if he didn't survive? What would she do? She just couldn't bear to think about it.

The officers agreed to let her go if they could question her further at the hospital. Kip was in charge of closing the store. Brandy agreed to keep the place closed until the police had finished their work, and Kip agreed to open it for them in the morning.

Alone and headed back down the freeway, she left a message for Tucker, and then she burst out in tears, flushing out all the pain and pent up worry all the way to the hospital. By the time she arrived, her eyes felt like her lids were made of cardboard.

This was not the way she'd expected this day to go. As she entered the Emergency Room doors, she began to find some of her courage. She hoped it would be enough for whatever news they'd give her. She said a little prayer before she approached the admitting desk and strained to keep her lower lip from wobbling, Taking a deep breath, she told the admitting clerk, "I'm here to see Steven Cook. Can you tell me what room he's in?"

CHAPTER 7

T UCKER HAD REMOVED his flight overalls, stowed his equipment, and repacked his chute and the tandem chute, double checking each fold twice. He felt the vibration from his cell and noticed he'd gotten a message from Brandy.

"It's me, Brandy. I'm on my way to the hospital. Scripps ER. Dad's been hurt, and they rushed him by ambulance. I'm meeting the police there. I have no idea how long I'll be, but I don't want to leave him until I know he's going to be okay. So I'm afraid I'll have to take a rain check on that burger and beer. Call me when you get a chance."

He dialed her back, sorry that he'd missed her call earlier. It had been nearly an hour. She picked up on the first ring.

"Brandy, what happened? Is he okay?"

"I don't know yet, Tucker. He was unconscious when they took him away. I'm waiting to find out if they'll let me see him. He's alive, and that's a good thing, but I don't know anything else. I wasn't able to talk to him. I don't know if he's still unconscious."

"But how did he get hurt? Why are the police involved?"

"It was a robbery at the store. They got the cash in the till, the contents of his safe, everything. The police are following up on a lead Kip gave them."

"Kip?"

"I'm sorry. He's dad's helper."

"So how did he get hurt?"

"Apparently, he was hit at the back of the head, and then fell. I found him on the floor near the cooler. He didn't look good at all, Tucker. Lots of blood. I'm worried."

"Of course you are. Listen, can I meet you there? I'm about a half-hour away."

"I'd like that," she murmured.

Tucker could tell she was trying to stay collected but was having difficulty holding herself together. Her breathing was forced and ragged.

"He's at Scripps you say?"

"Yes. I can call you if they take him somewhere else. But their ER and critical care is one of the best in the country."

"You got that right. Okay, I'll be there as fast as I can. You need me to bring anything?"

"Honestly, I'm not focusing on me at all. I think I'm still in shock. Just come. That would help."

Tucker stopped by his apartment, wanting to take a shower, but knew he didn't have time. He changed his clothes, picked up a pillow and blanket, threw a couple of waters in a bag, and headed up the freeway.

The sunset was a rosy pink, which sent a glow throughout the waiting room at the ER. His arms overflowing with the blanket and queen pillow, he scanned the seats and didn't see Brandy, so asked the desk clerk. He peered over the top of his bundle, since the woman was taller than he was.

"Are you family?" she asked, examining his armful.

"Yes," he lied.

"Well, hon, the daughter is waiting outside the treatment room. They're getting ready to take him up to ICU."

"How's he doing? Can I come in and wait with her?"

"Sorry, can't give you his status, but let me ask her if she'd like some company. I'm betting she would," she said, scanning the pillow again, squinting her eyes and smiling. "Can I have your name, please?"

"Tucker Hudson."

"I'll be right back." The heavyset nurse winked at him and then moved with the speed of a linebacker, disappearing around the corner. It wasn't every day

Tucker spoke eyeball to eyeball with a woman who towered above him. In a few seconds, the side door opened, and the clerk called out, "Mr. Hudson, this way, please."

Brandy was in the hallway, speaking to a uniformed female officer. She abandoned the conversation temporarily and ran to his arms. An instant before she collided with him, he dropped his load and pulled her to him.

"You holding up?" he whispered to the top of her head.

"Better now." She snuggled to press herself hard against his chest, wrapping her arms around him beneath his jacket.

"How's you dad?"

Brandy pulled away, biting her lower lip. "Haven't talked to the doctor yet, really. Dad's had a brain scan and some bloodwork and some other tests. They told me his vitals were strong, but I don't know anything else. Hoping someone will talk to me before they take him upstairs."

The female officer appeared behind Brandy. "If you give me just a couple more minutes, we can get my questions answered, and I'll get out of your hair. That sound okay with you?"

"I'm sorry." Brandy walked back to the row of chairs they'd been sitting at, remained standing, her arms still about Tucker's waist. Good as her word, the police officer finished her questions and then was gone within a handful of minutes. Brandy leaned against him as they sat down together. A male nurse had picked up the blanket and pillow and placed them nearby, neatly folded.

"So how did this robbery occur? They hold him up at gunpoint? In the middle of the day?" Tucker asked.

"We still don't know that. Don't even know how many of them there were."

"Your dad have cameras in the store?"

"Only for looks. They don't record."

"All this is appearing like it was someone who knows your dad. Knows his way around the store. Knows the routines."

"I think that's what the police are going on. But, honestly, I don't care about the money. I just want to be sure he's okay, without any major—"

"Ms. Cook?"

Dr. Harrelson shook her hand and motioned for her to remain seated. He extended his hand to Tucker. "I'm Dr. Harrelson. You the husband? Boyfriend?"

Tucker found himself stumbling for his words, a bit put on the spot. "Family friend," he answered grasping the doctor's paw.

"Now *that's* a handshake!" Dr. Harrelson barked, feigning injured fingers.

Tucker thought he'd been rather careful and wasn't in the mood for jokes. "Sorry, sir."

"Okay, well we have good news and bad news, Ms. Cook. We're not seeing much brain damage on the scan, and the wave patterns are normal. He's got a little swelling, especially in the back here." The doctor demonstrated on his own head, palming an area behind his right ear at the base of his skull. "There's probably some pressure, which also could be from blood pooling, but we will monitor that, and it doesn't seem to be increasing, thank God."

"That's good. So what's the bad news?" she asked.

"He's lost a considerable amount of blood, and he definitely has a minor skull fracture, probably a concussion as well. The next twelve to twenty-four hours will be the most telling, but we should know more once we see how he weathers this."

"Is he awake yet?"

"No, and right now, I'm not anxious for him to be. I think we need to watch him, let his body heal and stabilize itself. There's a chance we'll have to go in there to relieve the pressure, but the bleeding has been stopped. We're thinking the bones in his skull will heal on their own."

"That's good news." Tucker was feeling encouraged and hoped Brandy felt the same.

"I was able to contact his primary care physician.

Your dad's in remarkable shape for sixty-two. His doctor gave me his medical history. That's going to help us out a lot."

"So what's the plan?" Brandy asked.

To their side, they all watched as her father was wheeled out of the treatment room and down the hallway by two male attendants.

"His color is much better," she remarked.

"Yeah. We were a little worried when he first came in, but he's responding quickly. We hope that continues," Dr. Harrelson added. They followed Mr. Cook's gurney as it entered the elevator.

Tucker noted the strong jawline and the shape of her father's nose, indicating a strong family resemblance. His face looked relaxed. A large white bandage was wrapped around his skull down to the level of his eyebrows and ears. Tufts of graying hair stuck out the top where it had been left open, some of it still caked in dark red blood.

"So we're taking him upstairs, now," the doctor started. "He'll be in ICU, on the fourth floor, tonight. Once we get him situated, if you want to briefly come in and say goodnight, that would be fine, but no more than five minutes. He probably won't hear you, and he definitely won't respond. Just preparing you for this."

"Thanks, doctor."

"I have rooms upstairs, if you need a place to crash,

but honestly, it would probably be best if you just went home and got some rest. Nothing like sleeping in your own bed."

Brandy searched Tucker's face. "What do you think?"

"I think he's right." He knew his apartment was not more than five minutes away, but he was hesitant to suggest he take her there. He hadn't entertained a woman at his place in several months and was in the habit of trying to avoid it at all costs. He was trying to recall how bad the place was, since it would be Brandy's first impression of how he lived. Though a tiny niggling voice whispered caution, he found himself overruling it.

"I don't live too far. But if you want to stay here, I'm willing to sleep in a chair by your side. I've learned to sleep just about anywhere."

"You a Team Guy?" Dr. Harrelson asked.

"Former."

"That explains the handshake. So, you two talk about it and then let me know. Give us about ten minutes to get him all situated, okay?"

Brandy nodded as the doctor left.

"I think he's doing really great, Brandy." Tucker had never seen the man before, but in light of what he'd been through, he thought Mr. Cook was looking good. "If he's stabilized, no reason for you to get worn out trying to sleep here. Hospitals make me nervous. Just too much going on."

Tucker had an aversion to hospitals. Even when he'd broken his legs twice in combat, he demanded he be able to walk out on his own, whether in cast or crutches or both. The first time it was nearly impossible to navigate. He got good at asking people to get out of the way by swinging his crutch high above his head like a hammer throw. He even resumed his skydiving, until his LPO found out and put a stop to it.

"You sure it's no trouble?" she asked. "Do you have a roommate?"

"No roommate. It's sparsely decorated and probably not to your taste, but I guarantee the bed's great."

She smiled, slowly swinging her head from side to side. "Why am I not surprised?"

"There. That's what I've been looking for." He angled her chin up and kissed her lightly. "I wanted to see that pretty smile. Ready to go?"

"I want to see him first."

An ICU nurse accompanied Brandy to the expansive room housing several beds, most of them filled. Tucker waited against the wall, sneaking a peek through the wide open doorway. He was able to see Brandy sit in the chair provided, reach over, and take her father's hand. She spoke to him, but too softly for him to make out. A few minutes later, with a gentle pat on her shoulder, she was ushered out.

"How's he look?" he asked her.

"He actually looks comfortable, but the nurse told me they'd be on high alert all night in case something happened. It's amazing he didn't break his arm or one of his legs, the way he must have fallen."

"Someone definitely looking out for him," Tucker answered back. "Let's go."

He drove in complete silence the short ten blocks before he arrived at the gates to his complex. He was grateful he didn't have to ruminate any longer than five minutes over his choice to bring her to his place. He'd have been a nervous wreck. Putting it all out of his mind, he helped her climb down from his truck, tucked the blanket and pillow under one arm, and took her hand with the other.

The first thing that hit him when he opened his front door was that he'd never before noticed that his room smelled of man sweat. Her room smelled of lavender and other floral fragrances. Before he turned on any lights, he stumbled in the dark, picked up the clothes he'd worn skydiving today under the jumpsuit, and tossed them behind the closet doors. Before he could choose the right lighting, Brandy turned on the bright kitchen lights, exposing the sink full of dishes. It was over three day's worth, even though he ate mostly frozen dinners on a regular basis.

Why hadn't he thought about this?

He hung his head sheepishly, hoping it didn't leave too much of a negative impression. "Between house-keepers," he mumbled, rolling his neck and left shoulder.

"You already warned me, so no worries. You also mentioned you don't have a decorator." She smiled, seemingly to enjoy his squirming. "I wasn't expecting an extreme makeover," she said, batting her eyes at him.

Tucker was definitely not feeling the least bit romantic. He was scared out of his gourd. He was on uncharted territory and regretted not paying attention to that little voice that usually gave him pretty good advice.

She wandered around his living room, examining the walls and bare corners. He had one couch, and it conformed perfectly to the contours of his large frame, even if it was ugly as sin. The table in front was a wooden shipping crate. She leaned over it and studied his choice of reading material. Several nudie magazines with specialty titles like *I Love Titties* and *Booty Call* were stacked five or six issues deep. All he could do was close his eyes and wait for her reaction. It was too late to whisk them away out of sight.

She picked up one cover and showed him the enormous boobs on the unfortunate girl. "Do mine look anywhere like these?" she asked, her face showing no expression.

"Holy cow, Brandy. No. *Fuck* no! Yours are…well, they're just right. A nice, full," he began to hold out his palms, fingers splayed and pointing up, "handful, just overflowing."

She had her hands on her waist. It was one of those attitude things women frequently gave him. He knew he was in some trouble, but wasn't sure how much. With his lack of sleep last night, his radar was not working, and his blood was inconveniently pooling elsewhere. He hoped she didn't notice. He wished she'd say something.

"But completely inadequate, compared to these." She held the magazine up, covering her chest.

"God, Brandy, those are unnatural. I mean if I wanted to play with a couple of deflated basketballs, I'd go take a drive to Sports City."

She flipped the magazine over to examine it again. "They do sort of look like basketballs."

Since she wasn't smiling, he carefully waited for the whole scene to pass. He tried to reassure her he liked her just the way she was built.

"And you have lovely curves, sweetheart. She's like a human tuck and roll. I like nice, curvy hips. I mean look at me. I want a woman I don't have to worry about breaking her pelvis when I make love. I hate skinny women."

He wasn't sure it was enough, so he waited, squinting as if bracing for a blow. She tossed the magazine back onto the table, and picked up one of the big butt issues. "Big Book of Booty. Nice."

Her darting glance at him was painful, but his dick was having great fun at his expense. Luckily, Brandy didn't look there. Instead, she smiled and asked him, "Does my ass look like this?"

Tucker was stumped. Brandy's ass did indeed look like the cover model's. She was round in all the right places. He decided he'd have to live or die, but he'd be honest with her.

"Yes, your butt looks sort of like that, only better. Smooth as silk. I love the way it looks and feels, sweetheart." He was hoping she didn't catch on that this was his favorite magazine.

"So why'd you buy this other one if you don't like basketballs with nipples? Or are you lying to me?"

"Look, Brandy, we're going places we don't have to go. But the truth is, there are some nice pictures on the inside. They aren't all like this. This is shock value, to make men buy the magazine. That's all. This is like a cartoon, a comic book, something men do to pass the time, like playing a video game or something. It's all fantasy."

He carefully maneuvered himself behind her, removing the magazine from her hands and turning her around.

"I don't need those things anymore. I got the real thing right here. You were created perfect for me. I mean that, Brandy." He massaged the top of her spine. With the other hand, he slipped it around her waist and slowly pulled her to him. "Perfect, in every way," he whispered. He let his hands massage her ass, squeezing and pressing her against his hardness.

"Why can't I be your fantasy, Tucker?"

"You are. You totally are. Men look. That's what we do. You do it, I'm sure. I mean, I saw all those romance novels overflowing your bookshelf. Some of those guys were *naked*. I'm sure it's done to sell those books to women, right?"

He suddenly felt like a louse. Here her father was in ICU, and he was having this discussion about boobs and booty. His lust was driving the conversation, clouding his better judgment. It wasn't fair to her. It wasn't even fair to himself. He wasn't acting like a real man. He was acting like a wolf—and everything he didn't respect. He was disgusted with himself.

He stepped away.

"I'm sorry, Brandy. This isn't right. I brought you here so you could get a good night's sleep, to help you rest." He chanced stepping back to her until he could feel the heat of her body again. "Let's just keep things simple and do that, okay? Let's forget about all this crap. I'm beat, and I'll bet you are, too. Can we call a truce and just sleep? I'll even keep my clothes on if you like."

He could feel her soften as she bridged the gap between them, all those lovely curves fitting so nicely, making him come alive. She placed her palms on his chest.

"It was my fault, Tucker. But I think you have a good idea there. Why don't we just go to bed?"

"You're on. No objections here," he lied. He tried to keep his grin from looking too lecherous. He took her hand and gently pulled her to the bedroom. He pretended he didn't notice the posters of well-oiled ladies on motorcycles, stark naked, or how she was staring at them with interest. She approached the poster with the row of ten perfect asses. He heard her inhale and hoped she wasn't going to object. If she did, he was going to rip all of them off the wall and toss everything from his balcony to the pool level below.

But what she did next surprised him. She removed her clothes, giving him one of those looks that made him nervous. It was the thing that scared him most about women. He had no way of knowing what was really going on inside her mind. While she stood in her bra and panties, she undid the center clasp and allowed the magnificence of her breasts to shine in the moonlight, beckoning to him. He was holding his breath, mesmerized.

"I like your idea. Let's just sleep." She pulled back the sheets and slid her naked body under them, invading his man bed, defiling his private sanctuary that would forever after smell like her and bring back memories of what it was like to have her there lying next to him.

He hurried to discard his pants and shirt and then his red, white and blue boxers, turning to sit on the edge so she wouldn't see the enormous hard-on he had for her. She snuggled close, wrapping her arms around his upper torso and squeezing her lovely upper chest against him. She moved her head just enough so her lips touched his ear when she said, "And then maybe tomorrow morning you can fuck my brains out."

Tucker knew he was hopelessly flawed. But he also knew he was utterly hooked on this woman. And he'd only known her for less than twenty-four hours. This had never happened to him before. If he wasn't careful, he'd be taking her to dress fittings and window shopping jewelry shops.

It would be the end of his life as he knew it.

And he'd love every minute of it.

CHAPTER 8

A S THE DAYS and weeks flew by, Brandy's father recovered with only a slight amount of memory loss. He still had headaches that drove him to bed from time to time. He was able to identify his attacker as Jorge, his former employee. Although both the Sheriff and the San Diego PD searched, when they couldn't find him and he stopped reporting for meetings he was required to attend, it was assumed he had fled to Mexico. With his prior record, when he was apprehended, he'd be going away for a long time, since the assault caused injury that necessitated a hospital stay, and drew blood.

Brandy and Tucker spent time with Dorie and Brawley when they returned from their honeymoon in Hawaii. She also worked longer hours at the grocery, and assisted her father in hiring two more experienced clerks. She hired a professional organizer to work with her dad to get the office looking more like an office than a storage unit.

But Brandy knew she'd have to get another good job like she had with the ad agency. The rents in San Diego weren't cheap, and with Tucker staying over at her cottage so much of the time, she wanted to get someplace more private and not under her father's watchful eye. But she was in no hurry. She allowed her relationship with Tucker to take it's own path. The longer she was around him, the less of a difference their fifteen-year age spread made.

But today was going to be an important test of their relationship. Tucker had worked on her non-stop until she finally relented. She was going to allow him to take her tandem skydiving. Although she'd visited the glider port and watched him jump and land safely a dozen times, it did nothing to remove her fear.

"You just have to ignore it. Just like you did when you learned to ride your first bike," he'd told her.

"But I wasn't going to fall thirteen thousand feet if I had a mishap on the bike." She couldn't imagine she would enjoy falling through the sky, even with Tucker securely strapped to her back.

"Trust me, it doesn't feel like you're falling. It feels like there's a blast of wind coming straight from the earth, holding you up so you can fly. It really does feel that way, Brandy. You'll see."

The old converted bomber with the door removed

loaded everyone and their buddies up after some ground instruction. Brandy and Tucker were to be in the middle of the jump, since it was her first one. Several SEALs and former Teammates of Tucker's jumped solo, doing cartwheels and in-air formations. At last it was their turn. She stood at the edge of the door, barely able to see cars moving below. Houses looked no bigger than her pinkie fingernail. The air that blew back through the jump door was freezing cold.

She wasn't sure when she was supposed to jump, and worried she'd catch her foot or shoelace on the flange at the opening.

"When do we—" she began to shout, until she felt Tucker's weight behind her and effortlessly they were out of the plane and freefalling. As her heart rate began to return to normal, she realized he was right. It didn't feel like she was falling at all. It felt like the earth was slowly moving to reach out and touch her, but very, very slowly. He tapped her arms, signaling her to make a human "W" as she extended them out to the sides and spread her feet.

He kissed the top of her head and shouted, "Close your mouth. I'm getting slimed."

Her wonderment and awe had caused her to forget that little part of the training. "Sorry," she shouted back at the top of her lungs.

Tucker handed her the cord to the chute and together they pulled it, which yanked her straight up several hundred feet, or so it seemed. As the glider extended, Tucker steered them around in circles, even driving them through wispy clouds, soaring up and then doing high-banked turns in mid air. As she came closer and closer to the earth, the air began to warm.

He pointed out the border. "That's Mexico right over there." He also pointed out several other landmarks. The San Diego Bay appeared like it was a shallow bowl of silver pebbles as it glistened in the morning sun. She took his hand and kissed his palm.

"Thank you," she said to him in the quiet. It felt like the ride went on for an hour, that they would be suspended all day, but finally the ground began to loom large. She threw her legs out in front of her as they landed on Tucker's, collapsed and rolled together in the long grass, entangled in the chute.

Looking up to the sky, it appeared twice as big as before, and twice as blue. A gentle breeze rearranged her hair when her cap fell to the side. Tucker's face and beard was pressed to her cheek. "I knew you could do it," he whispered. But even that whisper had the deep raspy tones that made her whole body vibrate.

"Amazing," was all she could think to say in return, as she continued searching the blue spans above her. "It wasn't anything at all what I imagined."

"It's like a lot of things. Scarier to think about than to do. We do thousands of these jumps on the Teams. Twice as high. At midnight when you only have your night vision specs on. You see oceans of glittering lights and hope that they're harmless animals, not the eyeballs of the enemy."

"I could never do that," she answered. "But I can see you doing it. Must have been fun."

Tucker hesitated before he said anything at all, and then she couldn't make out the words. She left him to his private thoughts. She knew he missed the life, and would ask him sometime how he replaced the adrenaline he used to have coursing through his veins. She wondered if being a farmer, or a father or husband would ever be really enough.

"Come on, we gotta get up before we get overrun with the newbies." He pulled her up by the straps, unhooked her from him and from the chute and began gathering the colorful fabric, shaking out the blades of grass and small rocks. She noted how happy he looked, with the sun shining behind him, greying hair blowing in the breeze.

She touched his cheek, making him stop, his hand wrapped around her wrist.

"I mean it. Thank you, Tucker." She stood on tiptoes and kissed him until he swept her up and carried her off the field, the lightweight nylon chute tucked under his arm.

Afterwards, they went for a seafood lunch down by the marina. She scanned the million dollar vessels and the people out walking their dogs or jogging on this sunny Sunday. Every day was sunny here.

"See, you wouldn't have this in Oregon," she chided him.

"That's very true. This suits me."

"Me too."

Over their soup he asked her, "Where do you want to go for Valentine's Day?"

That sent a zinger up the back of her legs. She recovered quickly, but couldn't make a decision. "Anywhere. You just name it."

"How about we go up north? Several of the guys and some of the wives are doing a road trip to Sonoma. Can you get a couple of extra days off? It takes a day up and a day down. Gotta stay and do some wine tasting. And I understand you're proficient at grape stomping."

"In February? You know anyone who has grapes this time of year?" She wrinkled up her nose and then winked at him.

"I love that picture with you and Dorie."

"Ah, the good old days, when I thought I had a job." She allowed her voice to wander off.

"You want me to move in? I could help with the rent."

Brandy's pulse quickened as her stomach turned. "I was thinking I'd move someplace else." She drank her water and didn't look at him for a couple long seconds, not sure she understood how he'd take it. "And no, your apartment is completely out of the question."

"Why would you ever want to move? Your place is perfect."

"And it's right behind my father's house."

"So? You don't think he understands what we do all night long, Brandy? Come on. He knows his little girl is all grown up, with grown up appetites. Besides, I think he'd be relieved you had someone to watch over you when he wasn't there to protect you himself. Give him a break. Let him relax. I'll do the heavy lifting for awhile."

The "for awhile" stuck in her chest. But, she had it coming. The conversation had come to the edge of their limit on what was safe to discuss. They never talked about long-term futures. It was way too soon.

"I think dad likes having me around, but it's hard to make ends meet with what he pays me. It's like my life's on hold each week I stay there."

Tucker was quiet, and then he spoke down to the tabletop. "Why not look at it like you don't have to decide right now. If you stay there you'll probably make him happy. He gets to see more of you than most fathers get. You're not pressured to go knock yourself out trying to swim upstream with all the other people clamoring for a fat paycheck."

She knew there was more he wanted to say, but was finding the choice of words difficult. She reached out and took one of his hands. "And I'm hoping you wouldn't mind, right?"

His brown eyes saw everything about her. He saw her insides, how her heart was beating, saw all her uncertainty. Saw how grateful she was that they'd met.

"That would be an understatement." His thumb caressed her knuckles and she thought she saw traces of a blush. "Can I ask you a question?" he asked.

"Shoot." She inhaled deeply and braced for something momentous.

"If we did decide to move in together, could I keep just one of my posters?"

CHAPTER 9

TUCKER HAD SCHEDULED a fishing trip to Baja for early March, but that wasn't going to change his plans to take the road trip to Sonoma County. As they were preparing, he received an enormous rent increase, so Brandy presented him with a key to her cottage.

"You sure?" He was thrilled, but surprised.

"Nope. But I think it's time and I did ask Dad. You were right, he said he was relieved."

"Just human nature."

"So have you decided which poster will come with you?" He loved the way she teased him.

"I'm leaving them *all* behind. Why have an imitation when I've got the real thing?"

He'd been doing extra workouts with several new boys graduating in June, looking to enlist after the summer. His back and knees were bothering him somewhat, so he decided he'd take his time moving his stuff, do it gradually so he didn't send himself over the edge. For the first time in his life, he was feeling his age. He could still bulk up, and work all the machines at Gunny's even better than when he was on the Teams, but his agility and speed was lacking. He was stiff in the mornings and sometimes woke up with leg cramps.

But when Team 3 got orders to do a temporary deployment back to Baja, everything changed. The Team Guys were to work on the sex trafficking ring they had slowed, but now had flared up again. The fishing trip was still on, but Tucker was going as the real civilian, and it would be no picnic for the active duty SEALs. He'd gotten special permission after initially having his participation rejected. He was excited to be of service, even if it was logistics support, to the men he'd previously served with.

Brandy wasn't pleased.

"I think the Navy is using you as bait, Tucker. I mean, you have to pay for your part of the trip, but you don't really get to do whatever you want to. You have to hang with them. They should at least pay for your way down and back and the cost of the rental when you're there."

"I'm actually happy about spending more time with them than I would if it was a real vacation. We usually can only get two or three days, like our Sonoma trip."

But she didn't understand Tucker would have paid

anything he could afford just to be embedded deeper within the community. He knew it was a hard thing to explain, so he didn't try.

He was nearly settled with the move, just ahead of their road trip. He had so little furniture, only the closet revealed the secret of his residency. Brandy got rid of her bed. He got rid of the old couch. Everything else he left behind for a young recruit who was beginning his first workup in BUD/S—someone who also appreciated his stash of magazines and posters.

He offered to rototill the back lot for Mr. Cook as a thank you for letting him share the cottage with Brandy. He even offered to pay a little more in rent, but Cook wouldn't have any of that.

Tucker fixed the clutch wires on the "mangler", as he called the tiller, switched out the gasoline after installing a new gas tank and filter. The machine purred like a kitten. Afterwards, the sandy light brown soil looked like chocolate sugar. He imagined Cook would have a field day while they were gone, planting all his early spring seeds.

At last, they took off for Northern California, driving in one long caravan of ten vehicles. Their destination was Frog Haven Vineyards, where several of the SEALs had invested some of their re-up bonuses. Brawley told him it was run by the infamous *Pirate*, who had also been a member of Kyle's squad. Tucker had never met the man.

But he'd also been on earlier road trips when he was active and knew all about Nick Dunn's winery in Santa Rosa, which was on the way. His sister had left the property to Nick. He and Devon converted the nearly bankrupt nursery site into a world-class wedding center, lavender farm and winery. Tucker had been part of several work parties in past years, but had never seen the final result, and knew Brandy would love it.

After only two stops along the way and nearly ten hours later, they arrived in Sonoma County, not stopping until they got all the way up to Healdsburg and the famous Dry Creek Valley. Traveling the winding country two-lane freeway through the valley floor, they found it covered in blooming bright yellow mustard flowers between rows of blackened and gnarled old grapevines. Vineyard workers were cutting back last year's growth to make way for trellising new ones. The air was lightly scented by the smoldering piles of clippings and farm debris all along the way.

"I can't believe I've missed this area," Brandy remarked. "Never thought I'd find anything prettier than Coronado, but this comes pretty close."

"People come here from all over the world just to drive around, eat incredible food and taste great wines. Barrel tasting is really big in the early fall."

"Sounds like Heaven," she answered back.

"These guys have it good. Zak's nickname is the pirate. He got injured on his first deployment, shot in the eye and is real lucky to be alive."

"I'd say. But except for the eye, he was okay?"

"Yes ma'am."

"Were you close?"

"He came on board after I'd gone, so I never got to meet him. But after the injury, he wanted to come back. He worked like a dog and qualified Expert with his other eye, and went through most of the BUD/S training again. You don't find many guys who could do that."

"So he went back?"

"Well, Kyle wanted him back, I was told, but in the end, the Navy thought better of it and asked him to scratch. He met a local Realtor and they found this property and bought it, along with a whole bunch of Team Guys and their relatives. Now they're making beer, along with the wine. I hear it's real tasty."

"Zak sounds like one tough dude."

The caravan slowed down, the first car turning up a crushed granite drive, quickly disappearing from view. As Tucker began his approach up the driveway, he drove past a handful of mailboxes, and pointed out the winery sign.

"Frog Haven. That's it. Got the Bone Frog logo and

everything, not that the average tourist would know. You won't see a Trident anywhere."

They drove past more vineyard workers doing pruning and cleanup. A herd of small goats was grazing between several rows, hedged in by portable fencing.

"Am I seeing this correctly? Goats?" asked Brandy.

"They keep the grass down, leaving behind nutrients. A lot of the wineries in the valley are doing the same. Pretty smart. Rent-A-Goat." Tucker could see she was amused.

"No way. Really?" she asked.

"I don't lie. This herd is special. They make artisan cheeses the owner sells for big bucks. Your dad might even carry some in his store."

Once they approached the top of the swale, the jockeying for parking space began, with a couple of the big trucks nearly colliding. One by one everyone poured out, stretching and adjusting themselves after the long ride. In front of them was a quaint farmhouse with a large covered porch surrounding three quarters of the sides. It had been restored to perfect condition. An attractive woman in a smock apron, with two children hugging her legs stood at the entrance. Leaning against one of the porch posts next to her was a handsome man dressed in black, sporting an eye patch over one side. It had to be Zak. Tucker was looking forward to meeting him, finally.

Brandy shuffled over to Brawley and Dorie, striking up a conversation. Kyle's wife, Christy, ran to the porch and gave Zak's lady a big hug. A couple of the other wives did the same. Zak and Amy's two kids scattered into the vineyard to go play with a group of workers kids.

Tucker took Brandy's hand and they joined the small crowd that had gathered in front of the house, just as if Zak was going to make a speech to all of them.

Instead of Zak giving the speech, it was his wife.

"Welcome to Frog Haven. I'm Amy and this is my husband, Zak. I guess the kids are around here somewhere, so be careful pulling in or backing out of the driveway, *please!*"

The group chuckled.

"We're so excited to have you with us for a couple or three nights. We can sort all that out later. I don't think Zak has been able to sleep for a week, he's been so looking forward to your visit."

"Thanks you two," directed Kyle, taking charge. "Let's give them a big round of applause for making this one of the more frugal vacations we've been able to take."

The group clapped and several whistled or cheered.

Amy thanked them with a big smile. "Now, we have two unoccupied bedrooms here in the main house, but the bunkhouse sleeps twenty-four. No queen or king beds, so you'll have to put your singles together and negotiate the crack down the middle."

"Notice she said two beds together? No threesomes!" yelled Kyle.

After the laughter died down, Amy continued. "I'll let you sort all that out on your own. We eat in an hour, family style out back on the other side. I've got some heaters but there's no way I can feed you all in my little dining room, so wear your sweatshirts and jackets. If it's too cold for you, tomorrow we can arrange for supper to be served in the bunkhouse."

"Dinner attire?" T.J. Talbot asked her.

"Something you wouldn't mind getting stained with tomato sauce. We're going Italian all the way."

A cheer broke out, and as the crowd dispersed, Zak called them all back.

"Almost forgot. Short showers or only the first five of you will get one. My personal favorite is sharing, two-by-two. We have a nice hot tub you can take your time and soak in after dinner, if you like." Zak checked his cell phone. "On my mark....Go!"

The group took on the atmosphere of a church camp. The men were in sync because they were used to working together that way without anyone having to bark instructions. Tucker noticed several of the newer wives and girlfriends were completely confused, and

Christy was a big help with some timely advice, discretely placed here and there.

Tucker and Brandy selected a dark corner in the bunkhouse. Wire cables worked like stringers, attached with hooks to the walls in both directions so old sheets could slide into place, giving each couple some privacy like in a hospital room. Tucker moved their two mattresses together and then re-made the bedspread to stretch over both sides. He'd been told to bring some comforters, so he retrieved them from the truck, and added them as well.

At the opposite wall, there was an old Franklin potbellied stove and a generous pile of wood stacked halfway to the ceiling. Several rocking chairs made a semicircle around the stove for evening chats. Against one wall was a tiny kitchen with a sink, a refrigerator, a picnic table that could seat eight and a microwave toaster oven.

But the highlight of the entire bunkhouse was the bathroom, containing a two-stall unisex toilet and one shower. Tucker was looking forward to the hot tub after dinner to work out the kinks in his neck and shoulder. He doubted he could even fit in the shower, let alone share it with Brandy.

They washed up quickly and then joined the whole group outside on Zak and Amy's patio. Zak placed both their kids at the head of the table on a loveseat with pillows so they could see everyone. They were bundled for the ski slopes, wearing matching bunny hats.

At this time of year, the vines were bare, so the trellis they sat under left gaping holes where Tucker could see the stars. Some of the magic rubbed off when it turned very cold, with a slight breeze. He excused himself and grabbed their comforter from the bunkhouse and wrapped the two of them together while they devoured their steaming hot lasagna, green salad and a little too much red wine. With the slight buzz relaxing him, soon even the nippy night air stopped bothering him. He'd forgotten how different Northern California was from San Diego, where no matter what time of year, the temperature never fluctuated more than ten degrees.

Brandy was laughing at Christy's story of how she met Kyle, when she attempted to hold the wrong house open and found him naked and asleep—stretched out on the master bed.

Although the ladies were last to bond as a unit, as the wine continued to flow and the stories got louder and more daring, Tucker could tell they were already well on their way to coming together on their own team of sorts. It was important that the sisterhood of the wives and girlfriends stay strong and tight, since they would help hold each other up in case the unthinkable were to happen. Dr. Death stalked them all: men, women and children. And with the world exploding more and more every day, he was making house calls at home, in the good old US of A.

You son of a bitch.

Tucker had only had to hold one of his buddies as the young man's life passed from him. He never wanted to repeat the experience.

By candlelight, he studied the faces of those men he'd served with, and served under. He felt so lucky to have had that opportunity to be a grown up Boy Scout, doing crazy dangerous things, all the while making the world a safer place. He'd been able to push himself to his limits, the adrenaline nearly exploding from the veins in his neck, but as a force for good. Never evil. It was hard to explain to someone who hadn't experienced it for himself. It was probably the heavy wine, but right now he couldn't explain why he'd ever left. There just wasn't another job on the planet as good as being a Team Guy.

Amy put on some music and the ladies rushed to their feet to dance. It was fascinating to watch how women could just be so demonstrative, so ready to just throw their heads back, laugh and toss their cares over their shoulders.

Brawley scooted over next to him, and shared part of the blanket.

"You guys are getting along most excellently, my man. Brandy's a good influence on you."

"Nah. I still got the dirty thoughts, same as ever."

The two men chuckled. Brawley's eyes were sparkling in the candlelight as he watched his new bride dance with Brandy. Christy and several of the others became the girl group backup singers, line dancing in unison to the funky rhythm from an oldies satellite channel.

"We've missed you, Tuck."

"Missed you too," Tucker returned without looking at Brawley. "So you're staying in for another turn?"

"For now. Honestly, I don't know what I'd do if I didn't have this community or these things to do with my friends."

"I hear you." Tucker was trying not to dwell on it. He wanted Brawley to change the subject, but it was awkward sitting next to him, wrapped in the same blanket. He was sensitive about that sort of thing. As a youth, he'd probably spent more time with Brawley than he did his own parents.

"You'll have to hang around more when we get back to San Diego," Brawley said just before he finished his wine. Zak placed another opened bottle in front of the two men.

Tucker read the label out loud. "*Frog Haven Winery. A little piece of Heaven.* That's about how I'd describe it up here." He was hoping the change in focus would get the discussion off the Teams.

"First time I've seen it all built out. When they first bought it, I thought they were nuts." Brawley scanned the patio, smiling at the girls. "Now look at it. Piece of Heaven, indeed."

"Thought you invested like Kyle and Coop and everyone else," remarked Tucker.

"Nope. I bought a house with my re-enlistment bonus instead. Maybe the next time."

"So you're going career, like your dad?"

"I'm thinking PA school, or maybe med school, if I can get some tutoring."

"Geez, Brawley. You won't have any time if you do that. And you'll owe them another ten years at least."

"Well, it's a pipe dream." Brawley casually glanced at the ladies again. "They're getting smashed."

Tucker found this funny. "I think living here and doing this would be a whole lot easier. And no schooling or the cost of it."

"We'll see. First, I have to get in."

"By then, you'll have chipmunks running all over the place," Tucker reminded him. "Bills, gymnastics lessons and soccer practice. You ever spend any time with Kyle and his brood, or Coop? We can hardly get them to come out with us to the Scupper."

Tucker was convinced Brawley had forgotten his

earlier remark, until his friend cruelly drove the point home again.

"Hell, Tuck. What's stopping you? I mean Kyle says you're paying for a vacation chaperoning the Team all over Baja next month. Some vacation. Why don't you just re-up? Come back to us."

"Because I'm thirty nine, Brawley."

"So am I, nearly."

"But I've been doing other things. I'm just not sure I could get through BUD/S again."

"They'd have to give you a pass on that," Brawley barked.

"Nope. I already checked."

The two of them sat in the few seconds of quiet while the ladies searched for another station. In San Diego, there would be crickets on a night like this, even in February. Tucker had heard an owl earlier, but no crickets.

Brawley turned, speaking to the side of his face. "Well, you just confirmed what I've been thinking for the better part of five years now. Don't deny it, Tucker. You want back in."

He wasn't going to make a big objection to Brawley's remarks because that would make him look guilty as charged. But his friend had nailed him fair and square. That little confidential talk with Collins about whether or not the Navy would consider a re-entry for him was kept under wraps. But he had to go open his big mouth tonight and tell Brawley he'd checked. He wondered if he'd done it on purpose.

Wouldn't that be something if I could do it?

Brawley stood up and positioned the entire blanket around Tucker's shoulders and gave him a gentle pat on the back. "I think I'm going to go out there and rescue Dorie before someone gets hurt."

Tucker nodded. "Think I'll do the same," and stood to join him.

Brawley grinned like he'd been told a dirty joke.

"What's so funny?" he asked the newlywed.

"I think everyone's gonna get laid tonight."

CHAPTER 10

"WE SHOULD HAVE taken a week off, Tucker. I had no idea there was so much I wanted to see." Brandy was folding her clothes when Tucker made his way into their sheeted cubicle. He'd been stacking wood and making sure the fire was fully stoked so they didn't have to wake up in the morning to a cold building.

"Next time. I promise." He pulled her to him, fingering the red lace bra she'd bought for the trip. "Where on earth did you get this dangerous device?"

"You like it?"

"Turn around. Let me think about that for a couple of minutes."

She loved taking direction from him. She peered over her shoulder. "Like this?"

"Keep going."

Brandy slowly kept moving until she was facing him again. "Should I take my bra and panties off now?"

"I can't make up my mind."

His smile was bringing on a wave of hot, wet lust she could smell.

"Is it my imagination, or are these lovely lace things even more sexy looking when they're so—so—ample?" He darted a worried look her way. "Did I just make a huge mistake?" he said as he winced. He bit his lower lip and, in spite of his enormous size and white beard, looked like a little boy about to be punished.

"I used to let things like that bother me." She slowly slid her panties down her thighs. "But—"

"Don't touch that!" he whispered.

Brandy had her hand on the front clasp of her bra, ready to peel it away and stand before him naked. Instead, she splayed her fingers over the satin and eyelet lace, squeezed her flesh and took two little steps until their bodies touched.

"How is it that I'm always the one who's naked first?" she asked, her lips just barely touching his. She could hear his heart pounding in tandem to hers and took a gentle moan from him as they kissed.

"I guess it's because I always like to watch, and I forget myself," he whispered.

"I think it's healthy to forget yourself now and then, don't you?" They kissed again, but deeper. "You want me to leave it on or take it off?"

"I think you should leave it on for now. I'll get to it

in about an hour. I have other things I want you to do first. Is that okay with you, Brandy?"

She watched him remove his jeans and underwear, his erection bouncing with anticipation. She held him between her palms like she was praying.

"It's perfect."

IT WAS PAST midnight when she awoke, grateful Tucker held her tight because the room was freezing. Someone in one of the other spaces was snoring up a storm and would have rattled the windows if there were any.

Her heart was still racing from their urgent love-making. He'd played her body like an instrument, hard, and incredibly deep, expressed both in body language as well as their frantic whispers. It had been so intense, at one point she broke down in tears and Tucker thought he'd hurt her somehow.

But in a way he had. She was forever altered as if she was a willing participant in her own destruction.

It was hard not to notice a man as tall and strong as he was. But now that she knew him better, had kissed every inch of his body and answered his need with her own, she understood that everything he did he was the master of, except sometimes finding words. But he loved with abandon, never holding back, pushing her to the edge, and then just a little further, until she'd collapse in his arms. The coiled, cloud-of-butterflies-feeling in her belly were physical manifestations of what she knew to be true in her heart. She was falling in love, as she never had before. She also knew this came with risks, since there would be no getting over that kind of intense love. In fact, it was delicious and painful at the same time, even with the absence of a breakup on the horizon.

She tried not to think about where it all was going. She'd been included in the community of brothers, felt herself blend in with the ladies who were lucky enough to also be loved by one of these warriors who turned their worlds upside down. Brandy just took the waves of emotion and passion as they engulfed her and tried not to focus on what it all meant. She knew that was a rabbit hole.

It hardly seemed possible they'd known each other for such a short period of time. He'd been the missing piece she didn't even know she'd been missing. If she ever had to be without him, life would never be the same.

She thought about Amy and Zak, who was nearly killed on his first deployment. Shannon had lost her first husband, T.J.'s best friend. She'd also heard stories about the women who couldn't handle the lifestyle, the intensity of their play and their hearts. Still, it was a family, a community of brothers and the women they loved.

But one thing bothered her. Tucker had been talking with Kyle and Brawley, and she knew he missed being a SEAL. What would she do if he decided she wasn't the right one? What if he tried to re-join his team and failed? How could she ever make up for that incredible loss he would feel.

Or, what if she never could keep him happy enough to stay? Could she meet him halfway, match his energy, and carefully tend to him if he ever fell apart? She wasn't sure she was cut out for it, any of it.

Try to sleep. You have to rest. You'll drive yourself crazy with all these thoughts.

"Everything okay, Brandy?" His words startled her.

"I'm sorry, did I wake you?"

He sifted his fingers through her hair. "Yes."

"I can't sleep."

"That happens to me sometimes too when I drink too much. It's like I'm over-drunk."

She lay on her back and enjoyed the feel of his large callused hand caressing her breast. The plank beams on the ceiling were barely visible in the reflection of moonlight. Brandy waited, trying to notice some sign her eyelids were heavy and her mind was quieting, but that sign never came. She inhaled and tried to sigh very carefully so he wouldn't detect her worry. But even that was unsuccessful.

"Talk to me, Brandy."

"I don't want to do it here."

"Hot tub?"

They threw on some clothes and took their towels, discovering that they were able to be alone under the stars. The warm water helped Brandy put her thoughts into words.

She wrapped her legs around his waist and floated with her arms about his neck. The white in his hair and beard made him appear to glow in the dark.

"Is it that bad?" he teased.

"What?"

"Whatever it is you don't want to tell me."

"No, Tucker." She paused and thought carefully before she spoke. "Let me ask you a question. Does the speed of all this scare you just a little?"

"You mean does it fall somewhere between skydiving at midnight and getting my ass shot off by a sniper? That what you mean by scared?"

Now she felt ridiculous. "I got the impression you weren't the kind of guy who just jumped into relationships."

"Oh. Okay. So now we're talking *relationships*. Is that what this is?"

She would have been worried but saw the goofy grin on his face. "Watch it. Don't you make fun of me. I don't like that, as you know."

"Well, you're right about me. I don't do this. I've

never done this."

She didn't want to look at him in the eyes, thinking he might begin to get uncomfortable. The last thing she wanted to do was put him on the spot. But she wanted to know where she stood. And maybe that was the right way to put it.

"Tucker."

"Yes ma'am."

"Would you be able to give me some indication of where all this is leading? Like, do I fit into your life anywhere other than in your bed?"

He tilted his head and stared back at her without smiling, and her heart fell to the bottom of the hot tub.

"First, if you'd have asked me that about ten years ago, I'd be gone by now. Maybe even five years ago. But, believe it or not, I've mellowed. When I went to the wedding on New Years Eve, *my* goal, and remember I told you I didn't want to tell you what it was?"

"I remember."

"My goal was to keep my hands to myself and to not rank or otherwise check out the ladies at the reception."

"Okay. And how did that work out for you?"

"I didn't even come close to achieving my goal. I sat there in the church, and I watched as you walked down the aisle, and into my life."

Brandy was stunned. It wasn't what she'd expected

at all.

"I've been watching you when you were sleeping, talking to other people and didn't know I was looking. I watch you from across the room and out of the sides of my eyes when we go places. And I've come to the conclusion that I don't ever want to spend a day when you are not a part of my life."

She scrambled to her feet, separated herself from him and stood with her back pressed against the other side of the hot tub. Her heart felt like it was going to jump right out of her chest and go running down between the vines.

Tucker just waited. And then that grin overtook his face. "Oh my God. You're scared." He approached quietly, relentlessly, and without hesitation gently took her head in his hands and kissed her. "It's just like skydiving, sweetheart," he said between kisses. "You put your arms out to the sides, and fly. And I'll be strapped right there behind you. I will never let you fall. And I'll never stop loving you."

Thank you for reading this prequel novella New Years SEAL Dream. The full-length novel, **SEALed At The Altar** *is out now! You can order it by clicking* **here***.*

But just for fun, here are some answers to some of your

questions in advance.

Does Tucker decide to re-join SEAL Team 3? Yes.

Does he make it? I'm not telling! You're going to have to read it to find out.

Will they be together? The answer to that is a re-sounding yes.

He will never let her fall. And yes, they'll never stop loving each other.

I hope you will continue the journey of Tucker and Brandy. There's going to be a beautiful wedding in the story.

In wine country.

Happy New Year, dear reader!

Sharon Hamilton
Santa Rosa, California
January, 2018

But wait! Did you know that the Bone Frog Brotherhood continues! Check these out!

SEALed At The Altar, Book #2

SEALed Forever, Book #3

SEAL's Rescue, Book #4

But you know you gotta have more Brotherhood Books, right? Did you know you can buy Sharon's most popular series, the SEAL Brotherhood, in two superbundles? If you buy these, you can start right

from the beginning with Book #1, **Accidental SEAL**.
Even prequels are loaded into these bundles!

Ultimate SEAL Collection #1

Ultimate SEAL Collection #2

And just a reminder, you can follow Sharon on these
three easy steps:

BookBub

bookbub.com/authors/sharon-hamilton

Newsletter Signup

sharonhamiltonauthor.com/contact/#mailing list

Amazon Follow Me

amazon.com/Sharon-Hamilton/e/B004FQQMAC

SEAL YOU IN MY DREAMS

A Magnolias and Moonshine Novella

SHARON HAMILTON

CHAPTER 1

PETER WATSON WATCHED a human mermaid cavorting with the big fish in the Atlanta Aquarium. Her long blonde hair was pulled back in a ponytail and spread through the water like a giant yellow sea fern. Her shapely body was poured into a bright blue and yellow diving suit with the Aquarium logo on the right thigh. Her graceful movements took his breath away. She fed large angelfish and smaller shy bottom scrapers, making sure everyone got their fair share. Several sharks lurked in the background, used to the fact that they would not be hand fed anything.

He was transfixed. A class of grade-schoolers encircled him. He heard several of the children remark, "cool," or "I wanna do that some day."

As a Navy SEAL, Peter was familiar with wetsuits and diving equipment. He was used to seeing his buddies on SEAL Team 3 swimming like a pod of dolphin with their rebreathers, going undetected from the surface. He knew how to plant an underwater demolition charge, fire his H&K underwater with deadly accuracy, and use a submersible one-man sub. He'd done HALO jumps into shallow water and boarded ships operated by pirates and other assorted bad guys. But never had he played with a mermaid in a neon blue and yellow wet suit.

He felt like some hidden force placed a big hook in his heart and tried to yank it out of his chest. He noticed, as the children moved off to the next large window, that he'd been holding his breath.

Tyler and T.J. came up behind him, but he didn't notice. When T.J. barked, Peter jumped nearly an inch off the ground.

"Elementary, dear Watson. That," he said as he pointed to the girl, "is a thing of beauty."

Peter had to agree, once he settled down. All three of them stood in a line, about two feet from the Plexiglas window, drooling in sync.

She emptied the contents of her fanny pack, zipped it up, and waved to her gentlemen audience. The three waved back.

"Peter," started Tyler Gray, another SEAL from Team 3, "we got one night in Atlanta, and then it's back to San Diego. But if anyone can do it, you can."

"Do what?"

"Catch a mermaid," he whispered.

It was exactly what Peter was thinking.

T.J. motioned to a set of metal steps. Tyler and Peter followed behind him until the stairway veered off to the right, giving the audience a view of the tank from the top. At the left was a door marked private. T.J. glanced both right and left before opening the door quickly and holding it for his buddies.

"Wow, you know this place?"

T.J. stopped, causing Peter to run into him. When the big SEAL turned, his glib expression told Peter he was about to get a whole lot of attitude.

"Dude, I do know how to chase a filly. Now that I'm a married man, I live vicariously through you single guys."

"Like I need help with that?" challenged Peter.

"I'm positive you need help with that. But let's just say I'm selfish. Old married Tyler and I will help you get introduced, and then we bow out. Up to you to get back to the hotel by at least oh-nine-hundred. And you can't be wearing these."

T.J. referred to Peter's bright yellow aloha shirt, his green cargo pants, and the red flip-flops. And his orange toes, which one of the SEAL daughters had painted for him before they left.

His teammate didn't wait for an answer, faced the hallway in front of them, and took off in a brisk walk. A series of office cubicles with glass doors lined the hallway, until they hit the double doors, which automatically opened to the outside. There in front of them, the mermaid was rinsing off, and removing her flippers, her weight belt and fanny pack and had pulled off her facemask. Her hair was now free and glowing golden under the shower.

She placed a big fluffy white towel to her face and then popped her head up to examine them.

"Hello, fellas. What about the word private didn't you understand?"

"Ma'am," T.J. began, "we just came to see if you were okay. We experienced a minor earthquake down below watching you feed the fish."

Tyler couldn't restrain his snicker. Peter was still dumbstruck. The girl was muscled, with tanned skin and bright blue eyes. Her whole face lit up when she smiled. Peter wondered why she wasn't more afraid of three strange men watching her rinse off.

She laid eyes on each one of them and came back to Peter. "You let your SEAL buddies get you into trouble, or are you a frog, too?"

"Now how the hell would you know that?"

She reached out and pinched T.J.'s bone frog logo on his polo shirt, snagging his nipple at the same time.

"Ow!"

Without reacting to T.J.'s outburst, she removed Tyler's hat with the same logo, showing it to him. And then she pointed to the frog print tats on each of their forearms.

Peter extended his right forearm to show her he had identical ink. All the guys on Kyle's squad had those tats, all done by the same artist in Coronado.

"Well then, that explains it." She threw her towel around her neck and picked up her things. "Show's over, gents. I do the rest of it in private, and I have a job to go to in one hour, so adios." She gave a mock salute and just walked away.

"Shit, Peter. You're gonna be single at fifty if you don't get yourself organized," said T.J.

"You know, I'm a big boy, asshole. You don't need to lecture me." Irritation mounted. He was disturbed by the fact the lady didn't introduce herself—or ask them questions, like everyone else did when they discovered they were SEALs.

"I'm sure she'll like that a lot, but first, my man, you gotta get her nekked."

"I'm not—"

T.J. looked like he was going to punch him. "Yes, you are. You're thinking with your little head, and that's okay. We want you normal, not a priest."

"Oh, that's cold, man. You Catholic, Peter?"

"Hell no. And, no, I just want to get to know her."

"Hard to do that when you didn't even hardly say a word or try to stop her," added Tyler. "Just sayin'."

"Getting to know them is overrated," spat T.J. "We're here for one night. You barely have time for that drink I promised you. Don't forget it was your idea to go to the Aquarium instead of hanging out at Dante's."

Their conversation was causing attention and an older gentleman in a white lab coat with horn-rimmed glasses was making his way over to them.

"We were on our way out, sir. Thought we knew the lady," said Peter.

"Who? Abbey?" He turned and scanned the hallway behind him. "I didn't think she was still here."

T.J. walked briskly toward the doorway they'd come through.

"Have a nice day," said Tyler.

The man in the lab coat watched them leave without saying a word.

"Abbey. That's her name," whispered Peter as they descended the stairs. "I'm going to try something."

He approached the visitor information desk. A young girl stood behind the round command center desk and blinked nervously at him, quickly checking out T.J. and Tyler, who stood directly behind.

"Can I help you?"

"I'm Peter Watson, and we were just talking to Abbey upstairs."

"Oh yes. Abbey Hart."

"Right. She had to run off to work. We're underwater stuntmen working for a movie crew in town, and Abbey was giving us some pointers. We think our director might like to meet her." Peter paused, hoping his ruse would work. He tilted his head and gave her a crooked smile. The girl blushed. He lowered his voice to a whisper. "We've only got two more days of shooting, and I think Abbey could be in another James Bond film. Don't you think?"

"Totally! Oh, that would be so cool!" the girl gushed.

He was heartened. "You know where we might find her since she's gone off to work? My co-workers and I think she'd be perfect for the part. Truth is the actress we have slated will need a body double. Poor thing can't swim."

"Who?"

"Who, what?"

"She's wondering who the actress is," T.J. spoke up. "It's Brooke Decker."

Peter glared at T.J. He didn't have a clue who she was, and neither did the girl behind the counter.

"Playboy Miss October last year," added T.J.

"Oh. I see. Sorry, I just thought it might be someone famous."

"Tom Hiddleston is Bond."

"Oh, Abbey would be thrilled! She's always talked

about being a Bond Girl." The clerk quieted and then waited for another staff member to walk behind her. She whispered and leaned forward, addressing Peter. "I know she works at that place that is owned by the SEAL guy. What's his name?"

All three of the SEALs answered in unison.

"Dante."

BY PURE LUCK, Dante's was a well-known, local watering hole and big time SEAL hangout that grew into an Atlanta tourist attraction as the little bar expanded. Dante himself was one of the early Vietnam SEALs, who helped spawn the legend of the frogmen in those early days. He retired and did what a lot of the early SEALs did, opened up a bar. As his notoriety grew, Dante's transformed with the addition of a pirate ship, barbershop, ice cream parlor, and jazz club.

The SEALs had it on their agenda to give the old man a hearty ahoy. Although legendary in the community, he was also known for not talking about his service years. Now that they'd learned Abbey worked there, Peter had even more reason to show up.

A small jazz combo played on the stage to the side. A few couples were dancing. Tables littered the catwalks crisscrossing the hull and built around the ship. The whole environment felt like a pirate's lair on a lost island somewhere. Girls in pirate garb waited on tables and mounted steps with trays above their heads, carrying brews and food. It would be impossible to hear much in the way of conversation, and being a Friday night, the place was packed.

At first, they were told it would be an hour before they could be seated, but they were offered the long bar, called "The Plank," to forage for a seat or perhaps a table. They got lucky finding a table right away.

Peter was on the lookout for Abbey, scouring the room for her long blonde ponytail. They ordered beers and sat back to soak in the culture. Pictures of old SEAL Teams were plastered over the bar and even encroached across the mirror. Patches from various teams also were affixed, tee shirts signed, along with pictures of Dante with famous, as well as infamous, SEALs. The Polaroid picture of Saddam Hussein in his prisoner garb was copied and had a prominent place on the mirror, along with assorted other bad guys either caught or killed, their gruesome photos somehow not looking out of place. It was a watering hole worthy of any SEAL member, or family of one. All four bartenders were busy, big arms covered in tats and sporting mostly shaved heads or close-cropped hairstyles. No colored hair or fancy buzz cuts. The tats and ear piercings told all the crazy stuff. And, of course, the girls were tens or elevens. They came in all sizes and colors, but to a lady were gorgeous party girls of the highest caliber.

Dante knew merchandising all right, Peter thought. There would never be anything like this place anywhere else in the world.

T.J. recognized Dante from his pictures and invited him over to their table. The man's white hair and full moustache made him hard to miss. With his dark wraparound glasses, he looked more like an aging jazz or rock musician.

"You boys know your money is no good in here, right?" the infamous pirate boomed. Several tables nearby picked up on the conversation.

T.J. pretended not to hear him and shouted back, "Sorry, could you speak a little louder?"

Grins sprouted around the table.

Peter leaned to Dante's ear. "We met one of your girls, Abbey, at the Aquarium today. Is she working tonight?"

Dante nodded and scanned the room. "Not one of *my* girls, although back in the day, she would have been just the type."

The table chuckled in unison.

"You must be like a kid in a candy store, Dante," said Tyler.

Dante scowled and clutched his heart. "The old ticker can't handle too much of that, son. Besides, got a woman for over fifty years who satisfies me just fine. I like to look, but the bottom line is I'd rather come home to a hot meal and a warm bed than an empty house and a bottle. Get my drift?"

Peter nodded. True to the Brotherhood in general was the fact that fidelity, especially long-term fidelity, was prized in the community. Of course, not everyone could walk that line. Divorces were common, but a good woman was a prized possession and something to be cherished and protected. Peter liked that about Dante.

"I saw her arrive earlier. Pretty girl. You know her?" he asked Peter.

"Hoping to."

"She's friendly, but I think she's a good girl. She gets lots of attention, but always goes home alone, if you know what I mean."

"No boyfriend?" he asked.

"I never speak for a woman when it comes to the heart. And I never kiss and tell, either, though at my age, I have to be careful with the blood pressure."

"Understand you might be going on your second retirement," asked T.J.

"Sadly, yes, we're closing at the end of the summer. I'm going to miss it. But other ventures are calling me." He sipped on his mineral water. "Where do you guys head out to next?"

"We think Mexico, Baja," said Peter.

"Baja? Sure beats those long flights to Nam or South America when I was in. We always vacationed in Baja. Fishing."

"We go fishing, too, for bad guys," T.J. chuckled.

Dante's attention was piqued. "There's Abbey. Want me to get her to come over?"

"Appreciate the hand-up, sir," said Peter.

"Well, best of luck. I remember those days. I was blessed with a great memory, and I think I remember every kiss stolen at moonlight on the beach and every pretty girl I romanced. Every one." He placed his palms together and looked up to the ceiling in thanks.

Dante said his good-byes and walked unsteadily, holding on to the handrails all the way up to the top flight of his pirate ship. Peter watched him point in their direction, and Abbey nodded, giving him a kiss on his cheek. Dante waved in return at the SEALs then gave a thumbs-up when Abbey's back was turned.

She traveled the catwalks, switching back and forth, her hips swaying in a short print skirt like all the waitresses with a white blouse pulled down in gathers over her shoulders. Her hair was down, and the silky strands fell nearly to her waist.

She placed her tray on their table. "So this isn't really about a James Bond film, is it?"

Peter answered, "So your friend lied to us about having a way to contact you."

She looked at him like she was sucking on a lemon.

"Okay, we're here merely for the company," he admitted.

"Well, I spent this afternoon feeding fish. I guess I could stand to feed a few frogs. You want some calamari or were you after a heavier fare?"

"I think Peter here will eat just about anything you serve up, Abbey. And, by the way, I'm T.J. This is Tyler. We're both married. But this one?" He pointed to Peter. "No woman has chosen him yet, so he's single."

"Well, imagine that," she said, her smile broadening. "Thanks for the warning." She winked at Peter.

Abbey returned with a huge platter of fried calamari, along with roasted mild peppers and herbed sweet potato fries. "This is Dante's welcome platter. We think he gives away more calamari than he sells, but that's his business."

"You're gonna be out of a job soon, we hear," said Peter, reaching for a bright orange sweet potato wedge.

"I'm outta here soon anyway. Headed back to California. This is a summer job."

She heard a whistle, and her head perked up.

"Gotta go. I'll come check on you later."

"I like the way you say that," whispered Peter. He wasn't sure she heard him through the din until she answered.

"So how long is my watch?"

"All night, darlin'. We leave in the early morning." Peter stared into her blue eyes and felt the oceans move inside him.

T.J. and Tyler were slapping each other, but Peter was fixated on Abbey. He decided she had some special powers. She had to be a mermaid after all.

"I've never had a one night stand before." She winked at him.

"You lie," countered Peter.

"Seriously."

"Nothing more to say, other than I promise to make it memorable." He meant every word, pouring on all the charm he possessed. It was that important to him.

She shivered. "I'm bringing you oysters next." Her lithe body sashayed around their table and disappeared into the crowded room.

Peter felt like his heart had just dropped from his chest and was trying to flip flop down the plank of the walkway after her without getting stepped on or getting knocked off into the drink.

CHAPTER 2

ABBEY HART KNEW she'd be spending some long sweaty minutes with the handsome SEAL as she walked away from him. The hair on the back of her neck suddenly stood to attention. The tenderness of her flesh underneath was created by the extra blood flow her libido was pumping out. She needed a hot and sexy night to wash away the trauma she'd experienced over the past couple of months.

The move to California had been all planned. She was not only following Brian to his new job working in the family winery business, but she was also returning to Sonoma County where her mother and father lived. Until she found out that her fiancé had a different idea of marriage and long-term commitment. She'd never pegged him for a player. But he was, big time. And he was indiscrete about it, which made it even more painful for her. Everyone knew about his "side pussy," which was what the boys in his group called it. Even the girls understood that a guy *that* good looking had more options so of course he couldn't be faithful.

But his looks weren't what attracted her to him. It was the confidence with which he did everything, the mastery he had with people, his precision in putting projects together. He was much loved, a born salesman. And he'd ensnared her in his hooks.

She checked out the room at Dante's. The noisy background was something that settled her mind. All she focused on was taking orders and serving customers. She'd made friends with a couple of the other ladies, but every day she realized this was the perfect job for this stage of her life.

She didn't have to think about anything.

No, she didn't want any hooks or chains. Maybe some ribbon or silk ties, but nothing with any strings or long-term commitments. She was moving on with her life. She'd not been dating since their breakup. Especially after his drunken night of regret when he tried to charm her back to his bed and nearly raped her. Her self-defense course had worked, and that little bottle of pepper spray did the rest. She doubted she'd ever have to confront him again, and that was just fine.

She'd watched her mother wither and grow old as her father continued to run around on her—becoming a very poor liar up to when he stopped trying to hide it. On her suggestion, and after the breakup of her own engagement, Abbey had convinced her mom to file for divorce and agreed to move in with her.

That gave her an extra rock wall. No way she'd bring anybody home to the cottage in Healdsburg her mother lived in. And she'd planned to give her mother what she so deserved—someone to love and take care of her. It was an all-consuming job, leaving little time for anything else but work and school. Her mom had been battling her father's infidelities and cancer at the same time. She might have triumphed over one, but not both. Her mom fought, and eventually lost, her battle with cancer only a few months later.

Life isn't fair.

No one had grieved when her engagement was called off and she moved in with her mom. But moving on was harder than she thought it would be. So she decided she'd put her own life on hold, concentrate on her mom, and just start over later when she had time. After her mom passed, Abbey was suddenly free again. She finished her degree, got a great job at a small winery in Healdsburg, and took the summer job in Atlanta to escape the small town prying eyes of Sonoma County—where everyone knew everyone's business.

Tonight would be the first of many un-complicated hookups, she hoped. Maybe this SEAL could free her soul, and for that, well, she knew how to fuck a man's brains out. It might be the most honest exchange she could manage right now. That and a promise to go away afterwards.

Both of us will get what we want tonight.

She dove into the crowd, letting the noise and crush of bodies make her invisible, but she felt his eyes on her all the way until it was done.

ABBEY SWITCHED SHIFTS with another waitress, so she was free at midnight to meet him in the parking lot.

The witching hour.

Peter asked if she could drive since he'd had a few and his friends were going to dump him without wheels. That meant he'd be entirely dependent on her, which normally she didn't care for, but was perfect this night.

"So that means, if we don't get along, I have to drive you back to your motel room."

"If you're that concerned, we could get another room there."

"At the Roxy? No, thanks."

"What's wrong with the Roxy?"

"I'm guessing you got it on one of those online sites, right?"

Peter nodded as they headed for her cherry red Volkswagen. She clicked unlock on her key fob and climbed into the driver's seat, waiting for him to get situated in the passenger seat before she continued.

"Haven't you seen an abundance of well made-up, tall working girls there?"

Peter blinked a few times and revealed a faint smile. "I wondered about that. Wasn't my choice. The price was right."

The long look he gave her was the non-verbal come-on she needed. He focused on her lips as the space between their bodies grew smaller and smaller, and then they touched.

He smelled like cigars and Tequila, tasted a little salty, but, man, his humming passion synced perfectly with her own internal motor. She inhaled, careful not to show that hitch in her breath, and deepened the kiss, following his lead. With her heart pounding and the neglected space between her legs shouting for attention, she was headed into a full-blown swoon worthy of any big screen romance. The earth moved.

As they separated, he gave her an appraising gaze. "Now that's what I call a good and proper hello."

Her insides chuckled at the meaning of the word proper, and it must have shown, because he answered her internal thoughts with a lop-sided smile of his own. The dark blue of his eyes turned midnight black as he licked his lips and watched her crave him. It was so sexy to have a man watch her bloom and let all that female energy come busting out.

"I'm wondering how I ever managed to think about kissing before now, Abbey. You are world-class."

"And you probably know best, right?"

"I like to think my experience makes me more fun, honey," he admitted as he slipped her hair behind her ear. She was going to let him play with her as much as he wanted to. She thought of it as practiced meditation. Giving herself up to the moment without any of the what-ifs or what's nexts. She'd already decided that was the part about being unentangled.

Oddly, he reached for her hand and gently kissed her palm, all the while studying her reaction. "I like to go slow sometimes."

That was fine with her. But, man, her bud began pulsing, driving an electric current all the way up her spine. She almost ripped off her shirt right here in the parking lot. Instead, she let the fantasy warm her.

"Slow is good. Sometimes." Her voice came out in a croak. She extended her fingers to reach his cheek. Then she ran her forefinger over her lips. "I like being kissed slow sometimes." She felt him jolt inside, sending off a tiny vibration and knew he was exercising control. She decided to pour it on further.

"We have a few hours. We could do this here, or we could go to my place. There, I think you definitely would find the price right." She leaned over to her right and planted a neat kiss to his lips and then turned back to the steering wheel.

Peter made a great show of inhaling and then buckling in.

"I think I'd follow you just about anywhere." He didn't look at her, and she noticed he was adjusting his belt and some other things, as well.

He watched her nearly the whole ride over. Several times she peeked over at him, and he raised his eyebrows. "What?" she asked on one occasion.

"You're nice to look at."

"Well, thank the Lord." She was inwardly pleased, but tried not to show it. "I take it you're from the South?"

"Whatever gave me away, darlin'?" he replied in an exaggerated drawl.

"I'm a California girl, so I can't make out your accent. I need a little help."

"I can do that," he whispered as he traced a line from her ear, down her neck, and over her bare shoulder to where the white cotton gather hugged her arms just below. Then he slipped a finger under the elastic and stopped. "Am I warm?" he asked, teasing.

"Not sure about that, but you're definitely on the right track. Do you mean will I take my clothes off in front of you?" She looked back at him as he withdrew his fingers. "Not if you don't tell me where you're from."

"Very well. I'm from Tennessee."

"Ah, the man from Tennessee."

"That's me."

"Are you a singer?"

"Hardly. I can't carry a tune. But I do like music, and I love to dance. I just save my performance skills for other pursuits."

She wanted to know more about him, but all of a sudden became too shy to ask, before pushing it aside. "Are you east coast or west coast?"

"West. I'm on SEAL Team 3 out of Coronado. Had never been to California before BUD/S."

"Ah. My Golden State."

"I knew you came from Cali before you told me."

"Who talked?"

"You did, darlin'. I could tell from your inflection. You've got that California accent that's unmistakable."

She'd heard it before, but never believed it. Her whole world sounded just like she did.

At her apartment complex, she wound around the night landscaping lights, coming to her building of four units, and climbed the wooden steps, feeling the heat of his body behind her. After inserting her key, she turned to face him.

She wanted to remember the excitement of his face so close to hers, the look in his eyes before they'd done anything but kiss and tease. For some reason, it was important, like a marker in time along a roadside with a whole lot of unmentionable ones to come. His would be the face at the doorway of the new Abbey. The carefree Abbey, the unwounded Abbey. And she'd use his attraction to her to heal the fissures and roughness in her soul, to make-believe that life was perfect and someone could love her absolutely without regard for tomorrow, even just one night.

He showed an honest face, but she still felt the skepticism niggling at the back of her brain. Her track record sucked when it came to her choice in men. But there would be time to think about that tomorrow. Tonight, if she could allow herself to trust, she'd know that she was still human. She'd get reacquainted with the old Abbey who could fall in love, throw caution to the wind, and forget how much it hurt to believe in those who let her down.

It was, after all, what she needed to do. Move on.

He frowned. "You okay? Something wrong?" He didn't touch her or place her hair behind her ear like she knew he wanted to.

"I'm coming to this, collecting myself from a bad experience." She was surprised the words escaped before she could stop them.

Damn!

He stood straighter and glanced around. "And are we going to be interrupted?"

She giggled, looking down at her feet.

He tipped her chin and lifted her face to his. "I'm serious. I don't want to tread where I shouldn't. You married? I don't poach on another man's kingdom."

She allowed the strength in his fingers to steady her, forcing her to examine his dark eyes. "What I meant was that I was engaged. *He* threw it all away, not me. I got out with my dignity, and not much else."

The faint nod he gave her and the twinkle in his eye made her knees buckle slightly. If he hadn't slipped an arm around her waist and pulled her tight against him, she'd have collapsed. He kissed her, whispering back, "Then let's get that thought out of your head, sweetheart. Because, whoever he is, he's one dumb sonofabitch. I'm here to prove him wrong."

God, she needed to hear that! She needed the taste of his tongue in her mouth, the way his lips pressed against her teeth, and to hear his hoarse breathing and the hitch and groan of a man in need as her hands traveled to the front of his jeans. He kissed her neck then across her shoulder and pulled down her blouse, exploring closer to the top of her bra. If anyone could do this, he could.

She slipped from his grasp, turned, and fumbled the door open. He shut it behind him and began the slow, relentless walk toward her that would change her life forever.

"Swear to God, Abbey, I wanted to go slow, but now I'm not so sure. Forgive me if—"

She stepped to him, slamming against his chest, kissing his neck, unbuttoning his shirt, and then pulling up the tee shirt underneath. Her fingers were headed for the buttons on his jeans.

"Doesn't work that way, darlin'. I don't get nekked before you do. That's not the way I do things."

"So let's do something different then."

"No, we're gonna do it my way."

She kept unbuttoning his fly, yanking on his shirt and tee shirt. His chest was bare, revealing in the moonlight a well-muscled torso, huge shoulders, and a six-pack as well-defined as any underwear model. He swatted away her hands as he removed her blouse and tried to spin her around to get at the back of her bra. She grabbed his hips at her sides and slid his jeans off, taking his boxers with them. But he still had on his cowboy boots, which presented a problem when he tried to step toward her to yank on her skirt.

He nearly fell against her. But he was the first one naked. She slipped out of her skirt and removed her bra herself. With his pants around his ankles, they fell onto the bed. Abbey was on her belly with Peter smoothing over her rear, probing for her opening. He bit her shoulder, then grabbed her hips and pulled her to him.

She extended her tailbone into his groin and parted her thighs. In seconds, he was inside, pulling her up from the bed, gripping her hips, and holding her tight against him.

She felt the same desperation he acted out, the need for him to be as deep as possible, to plunder and plow through her soft tissues that had been neglected for so long. His short breaths and deep thrusts sent her bud pulsing. She removed his hand clutching her right breast and placed it between her legs, holding two of his fingers against her nub and pressed.

It all came rolling back, the need to be devoured, the need to drive the other crazy, the need to take and give, to fear her heart would burst with that blissful feeling that nothing in the world mattered except how deep his cock was seated inside her.

CHAPTER 3

P ETER WOKE UP before sunrise when the blush of a new day was upon them. Abbey had curled up under his arm, her hands tucked beneath her chin, her thighs like a vice hugging his knee, which pressed against the damp softness between her legs. She slept silently, and for a time, he thought perhaps she was awake, she was so quiet.

Her skin brightened as the morning sunlight illuminated everything, turning her hair into strands of pure gold. He could watch her forever.

They'd been sent to Atlanta for some training on pain with amputees. T.J. had begged for the spot since Coop was staying home, and he recruited Tyler and Peter to be cross-trained, to have a backup specialty, as was the case on all the SEAL teams. T.J. was the official medic on this go-around, but everyone on Kyle's squad had to know how to fill in, in case Coop or T.J. was incapacitated. That was the strength of their team.

Tyler was also a crack shot and worked with Armando, who were their No. 1 sharpshooter.

But today, he didn't want to do anything with his team. He wanted to stay in this bed with this lovely lady he'd pleasured all night long until they both nearly fell asleep in each other's arms, giggled, and called it quits. That was a very nice way to fall asleep. He'd pay for it later.

His phone rang, and he panicked, thinking for a second that perhaps he'd overslept. Had he fallen asleep with his eyes open, just staring down at Abbey? It was T.J.

"Change of plans, Pete. We've got another two days here."

"What happened?"

"They want us to interview some aid workers who work with runaways. Some of them are working with girls smuggled into the US from other countries. Kyle wants us to see if we can get any information on the Garcia cartel from Baja."

Peter had been whispering, but now Abbey was fully awake, kissing his stomach, his belly button as she crawled on top of him and started to rub her sweaty and sweet-smelling self all over his lower body. When she finally did glance up, her eyes were molten.

"Uh, okay then, T.J. Another two days it is." He gave Abbey a wide grin, but his buddy was still on the line. He gasped as she squeezed his balls and stroked his length. Her lips found him, and within seconds, she was riding his thigh while swirling her tongue around his rod and making him forget he was on the phone.

"You still there, Peter? Something wrong?"

That's when he realized T.J. had been filling him in with details he'd have to repeat.

"Um, yea."

She had him all the way to the back of her throat and sucked hard.

T.J. chuckled. "I figured you'd be occupied, but also thought you could use a few more hours of shuteye. Can you get your ass over to the Pancake Hut by our motel? Say by noon? Can you do that, dragon breath?"

"I think I can do that," Peter whispered, barely able to control himself.

"You want a wakeup call in a couple of hours just to make sure?"

He couldn't think. She was working so hard on him, and his cock felt huge lodged deep down her throat. He was mesmerized by the sight of her lips devouring him, her cheeks sunken. Her little moan nearly made him explode.

"Gotta go now, T.J. Talk soon," he said quickly in a helpless whimper, taking careful attention to turn off the phone before dropping it on the carpet beside the bed.

"Holy smokes, honey! Where in the world did you learn to do that?" He sucked in air and then tried to lie back, but he was full into the action.

She kept her focus without smiling, which Peter appreciated.

IN THE SHOWER, Abbey proposed he and his Teammates show up at the Aquarium after their interviews.

"And do what? Chase you around the tank?" Peter was rubbing shower gel all over her chest then smoothing it down her thighs.

She returned the favor as the shower water rinsed her back. "Come talk to the kids. We have a Jr. Nature Club meeting today, since it's Saturday. The kids get to watch all sorts of films on fish hatching and sometimes cleaning bones and shells brought in by Scientists who are studying the ecosystem. You could tell them what you do, if you're comfortable with that. Since it involves underwater diving, I think they'd enjoy it."

"You want me to talk about cleaning your bones, making you cum a dozen times, that kind of what I do?" he whispered.

She raised her right shoulder like she'd been tickled behind her ear. "No, silly. They're just kids."

"Well, how do you think they got here, missy? And as for cleaning dead fish and picking over bones, well—" He drew her thigh up over his and tickled her sex. "I'm suddenly hungry!"

She stopped him from going to his knees.

"I'm serious, Peter."

He watched her expression and couldn't tell if she was playing with him or not. Part of her looked so innocent, and that other part looked like it was bustin' to get loose.

"Whatever you want, honey. I'm all yours." He stepped back and let a good foot come between them.

"So you think you can escape? Is that what's going on now?" she delivered with a smirk. Her eyes dropped to his dick, which was very interested despite the lack of attention. His blood pulsed quicker as she licked her lips.

"Oh hell, come here!" He grabbed her, slid his fingers up the back of her neck and scalp, and sucked her tongue deep into his own mouth. She tried to pull away, but he wouldn't let her. She finally moaned into him and deepened her connection. When they parted, he felt like there was steam coming from his ears.

"Wow."

She moved back into the water and smiled, inviting him.

"Since I have obviously no choice in the matter, when would this be?"

"About four to four-thirty. You don't have to take up the whole half hour."

She turned around to rinse off her well-soaped chest, and Peter washed her backside, using the opportunity to drop the gel, rinse off, and slide along the fold in her behind.

"I see. So you want me to talk about what we love to do, is that right?"

She nodded.

"Like this?" He plunged deep inside her and heard the satisfying hiss of her inhale across her teeth. "Oh God, Peter."

Once he was fully inside, he pressed her against the tile wall, lifted her right thigh, and rode her from behind, demanding to go deep. He stroked her slick insides, pulling her down on him hard.

With the water still running after several frantic minutes, he felt her melt against him, clutch his thigh, and angle back into him, her head resting backward on his shoulder. She was whimpering.

"Morning, sweetheart," he whispered. "I've sort of got a one track mind. I can't seem to get enough."

She groaned the deeper he got, balancing her body by pushing against the wall as he thrust several more times until he felt the familiar spasms tearing through her lower body. He picked up the pace, causing her explosion. She stilled at their point of climax, holding fast until she could no longer do so. Letting go, they writhed together. Peter kissed and bit the back of her neck and shoulders as their entwined orgasm became one.

Their breathing slowly returned to normal. He kissed the sides of her neck, down along one shoulder, the top of her spine, and down several vertebrae. He rubbed her thighs in long strokes before slipping one hand between her legs from the front to pinch her bud, causing her to jump. She limply leaned back on him, draped her arms over his, and groaned as they separated.

He turned her. With the shower spraying to her right, she did look like a mermaid. Her blue eyes called to him under the ribbons of water making her tanned skin glisten. He sucked her lips and feasted on the flesh under her chin.

His one-night stand had suddenly become very, very complicated. And he liked it that way. He drew her face to his chest, wrapping his arms around her warm body, and held her tight under the water.

"Thank you, Abbey."

She was all smiles when he released her. "So will you come speak to the kids?"

"How can I say no? Let me check with T.J., and if we have time, I'll make sure we're there."

"Perfect."

SHE DROVE THROUGH an espresso stand, bought them

both a latte, and headed for the Pancake Hut.

"This is just what I needed," he said as he held up his coffee cup. She had placed hers in the cup holder between them.

"Good. They make the best coffee here."

"So when do you have to be at work?"

"Two."

"Wanna join us at the Hut?"

"I have pancakes and I'll not be able to fit into my wet suit. I try to go light before I have to dive in there and feed the fish. You know they can smell food on you, right? Confuses them."

He rubbed her exposed thigh with his left hand. "I do understand how they could get confused. Happens to me, too."

She was light-hearted this morning. He hadn't asked her anything about who she was or what she was doing with her life. He'd figured he'd have time for that later, but they spent every minute of it making love. It was totally the opposite of what he'd told T.J. and Tyler he was going to do.

"So you work at Dante's tonight?"

"Nope. I get off at five-ish. How about you guys come over tonight and I'll cook you something good?"

"I'd like that. I'll ask them. Not sure if they have plans."

"Can you stay over?" Her eyes sparkled as she tilted

her head forward as she asked the question.

"I think I could be persuaded." He winked back at her.

She dropped him off at the Hut and sped away as Peter entered the restaurant. It began to hit him how little sleep he'd had. He slid into a booth next to Tyler, facing T.J.

"Holy shit. Should I memorialize that look?" T.J. burst.

"What look?"

"That fucked to submission look all over your face. You can't even stand up straight. You kind of creep along, trying not to fall. Like your dick has turned into that fuckin' DOR bell."

Tyler was laughing at T.J.'s comments. Peter wasn't sure he liked them.

"Ding ding," Tyler chimed.

"You're jealous. That's all. You married guys gotta wait a couple of days. But I know you both, and you're not foolin' me one bit."

"Happy for you, man," answered Tyler.

Peter felt a bit awkward before he realized he was so sleep challenged he could hardly think straight. It was just like in BUD/S on Day 4. He shook his head, then decided to pour the cold water over his scalp, and shook it off, sending water all over both T.J. and Tyler.

"Douchebag." T.J. stood and brushed off the water,

but Tyler was a captive audience and couldn't get out.

Tyler emptied the contents of his water down Peter's back, ice and all. He hated how it felt, but he deserved every ice cube.

"Stop it, children!" T.J. barked as he sat down. "Can't take you kids anywhere."

The waitress arrived and began quickly rubbing down the table with a white towel. "You fellas ready to order or you just gonna mess up my diner?"

"We're having pancakes. Your best. Big fat ones," T.J. said.

"Eggs? Bacon? Sausage? Toast? Cinnamon rolls?"

"Keep going," said Tyler.

"You want me to bring it all?" she asked.

"That's right, darlin'. Gotta do something to make up for you having to work so hard to keep us entertained. We're sincerely sorry about the mess." T.J. turned on the charm.

The woman left, her shoes squeaking. She was sporting a wide smile, though.

Peter decided to get some of his questions answered. "So, T.J. what's so important about these workers? And how many days are we here?"

"Until further notice. We're getting intel for our next trip to Baja. We got three different groups we have to interview. I've only been able to set up one. One of the directors is in Mexico now and won't be home until

Monday. After that? It's up to Kyle."

"He's sure these workers know Santiago Garcia?" Peter knew Garcia's brother had been killed in a raid the SEALs had been involved in before Peter joined Kyle's team.

"That's what we're here to check out."

Peter downed the tall glass of orange juice. He tried to think about the human trafficking angle, which made him sad, but his mind was really on Abbey. He couldn't wait to get distracted again. His biggest problem now was trying to stay awake until then.

"Oh, almost forgot. We have an invitation to dinner at Abbey's tonight."

"Nice," answered Tyler.

"I'm game," said T.J. without a moment's hesitation.

"And we've got a speaking engagement at the Aquarium at four o'clock. Talking to kids about what we do. A little community outreach."

"I'm cool with that," answered T.J.

"She actually wants us to come back there? Wouldn't she rather have a little alone time with you?" asked Tyler.

"Well, it's part of her job. They got a Jr. Scientist club or something there, studying fish and all things underwater. She even took them on a field trip to Dante's, before they opened, of course." Peter could see his two buddies were genuinely interested. "She's at work until after the class."

"I think we could make it by four," added T.J. "One of those guys we visited at the center wrote a children's book on SEALs. He gave me a copy. Maybe the Aquarium could start selling them in their store."

"Yeah, bring it along."

"You sure you want to share precious lady time with us?" asked Tyler again.

Peter was starting to lose his patience. He noticed his lack of control was proportionate to his lack of sleep. "I'm not sharing, asshole. I'm giving her a little time to decide if she wants me for more than just a one-night stand. So you guys better be on your best behavior."

CHAPTER 4

B EFORE ABBEY GOT to the Aquarium she got Peter's
text saying they'd be at the talk this afternoon at
four. And she was thrilled he said they were looking
forward to some home cooking.

She checked the time and decided to make a quick
trip to the store before work. She grabbed fresh fruit
for a salad, four thick New York steaks, some fresh
string beans, and a couple bottles of her favorite red
wine. She chose one from a winery owned by some
SEALs near the one she'd be working at. The label had
a picture of a frog skeleton, and she thought it appro-
priate for tonight's feast.

She placed her groceries in a zip up cooler bag she
carried with her everywhere. When she arrived at
work, she placed the bag inside the walk-in cooler the
scientists used for preserving tissue samples and
storing works in progress.

Although she felt the effects of her lack of sleep, her

happy mood boosted her stamina. The churning in her stomach felt like love. It was always the same way with her. The non-attachment principle she'd held onto came crashing down, and in its place was a bright new day filled with possibility. Being around Peter had been a welcome distraction. Now she knew it would be hard to let him go.

She cleared all that out of her mind as she put on her wetsuit and gear, picking up a baggie of fish parts and chopped squid that the biologists portioned out for this afternoon's feeding show. With no special instructions on watching individual species, she readied herself, applied the fanny pack with the food baggie, and dove into the tank.

Saturday shows were busy, and she was a whole two minutes late, so quite a crowd had developed. She swam over to the large blue-green plexiglass window and waved at some of the smaller children, who waved back. She motioned for others in the crowd to come forward, and slowly, the front two rows of audience filled with little faces pressing to get the best view of the tank contents.

One of the biologists had named the large male whale shark in the tank Crestor after the cholesterol drug. He looked especially hungry today, and she made a note to have him fed earlier than normal and would request an increase in his calorie intake. Her tag wand had a tiny electric shock to it, which she retrieved from her belt when he got close and was persistent. Showing him the yellow tip of the wand was all he needed, and he meandered to the corner to await his turn.

With Crestor out of the way, she began stringing out parts of fish guts, keeping one eye on the grey shark. A couple of Blue Runners made off with a long tendril, pulling at the pieces until both swam away with a nursery school of Blue Tangs following behind. She carefully fed the pairs of Butterflyfish, who daintily ate from her gloved hands. A school of Yellowbanded Sweetlips plucked at pieces of meat that had floated to the rocky bottom, their bright, neon yellow lips smacking up the yummy substance.

With her food half-distributed, she examined her audience and waved again. The back row contained several tall men, and she squinted, trying to determine if perhaps the SEALs had arrived early. Going from face to face, she didn't recognize anyone until she suddenly saw the face of her ex-fiancé, Brian.

She blinked several times, not sure she was seeing him correctly, and when she last focused on the line of adults, he was no longer there.

My imagination is playing tricks on me again.

Though it had been over a year since she'd seen her ex, her mind had been playing tricks on her all summer long. She'd get a funny feeling and turn, not finding anyone standing there, but sure he'd been there nonetheless. She thought she saw glimpses of him peering around a wall or in crowds at the shopping mall, only to look again and see nothing of the sort. Each time her heart began racing. Today was no different.

No way. He doesn't even know where I am.

She'd heard the rumors of his new love interest and had been so grateful when she stepped on the plane in San Francisco, headed for Atlanta and the rest of her life. They had wineries, too, in Georgia. She noted that if she had to abruptly leave California she was certain she could get work there.

She finished the rest of the feeding, double checked a repair that had been made to the coral reef, which seemed to be holding, glanced back at her audience, and took a bow. There was no sign of Brian anywhere.

The warm shower afterward was one of her favorite parts of her day. She shampooed her hair, put on her jeans and her light blue Aquarium logo tee, and took extra care with her makeup. She even added a tiny bit of perfume then headed out to the showroom to give guided tours before the scheduled Jr. Nature Club event. Several groups of children on an exchange program came through with their sponsors. Abbey worked with translators to point out all the fish in the tank and show them pictures of what she did.

She kept searching the crowds for Peter's face, halfway feeling like he'd jump out and surprise her. Her senses were heightened. The closer it got to four o'clock, the louder her stomach growled.

She convinced one of the college interns to help set up chairs in the meeting room just off the main lobby with glow in the dark murals on the curved walls that bordered the big tank. She checked the projector and the film reel she always played, which told the little visitors what kinds of opportunities were available to them during the rest of the summer months. The lights were set low, and soon her young audience started filling up chairs, being directed by the reception area and another intern dressed in a fuzzy shark costume. "Crestor" was always a hit with the little ones. Occasionally, they hired a magician to dress up in the costume and do magic tricks with the young audience.

She began the film clip and adjusted the dimmer again, setting the room darker still before backing into a corner to wait.

"Hey, Abbey, how you been?"

Brian's voice sent an electric bolt down her spine. Whipping around, she saw no one behind her. Due to the structure of the room, his voice had been thrown from across the sea of chairs. She could barely make out his form, leaning against a painted Roman column from an underwater scene, but the way he folded his arms over themselves and crossed his legs would identify him anywhere. His forehead and eyes were bathed in dark shadow, and she had a sudden sense of doom. His unannounced appearance in Atlanta, after she'd been very careful not to tell any of his friends where she had gone, was not a welcome sign. It had been over a year since she'd last seen him.

She stood straight, her hands flailing at her sides, the laughter from the children underscoring that sinking feeling in her gut that he was here for nefarious purposes. He untangled his long limbs, stalked around the last row of chairs, and headed directly toward her, stopping an arm's length away and just staring at her.

"You had no idea how hard it was to find you, Abbey."

Oh yeah, you sonofagun. I did that on purpose.

Now she wished she'd decided to not return to Sonoma County. Her new employer would be the only way he could have gotten the information about her whereabouts.

"You could have tried to track my cell phone," she said as coldly as she could deliver.

He tilted his head, as if deciding which view he liked better, then righted himself and smirked. "I tried that."

Another shard of panic coursed through her body. Being on Brian's radar wasn't healthy for any living thing. She was now more convinced of it than ever. Why she had never seen this dark side of him before, she couldn't figure out. His practiced charm had masked what she now saw as his true nature. She'd held off reporting him to the police because of his veiled threats. Then she'd been consumed with her mother's care. Finally, as she learned of his new love interest, she didn't see the need any longer and just went on with her life, hoping to never run into him again.

But now she saw how lethal he was. His dangerous eyes spewed hatred. How could she have ever loved such a man?

"Well, now you've found me, so you can go right back to the pit you crawled out from."

He tented his eyebrows in a mock sour expression. "Wow! Not even a little bit happy—or maybe 'happy' isn't the word. Flattered?" He leaned back to see how well the words hung on her bones and shook his head. "Whatever! Not one bit curious why I worked so hard to find you?"

"Not really, Brian." She got hold of her stomach and felt her spine develop a firm straightness. "Now is not a good time. I'm working, as you can see." She pointed to the audience of rapt children.

"I'd like to take you to dinner tonight."

"Sorry, she's all tied up." Peter's deep soothing elixir of a voice quickened her heart. She wanted to kiss the ground he walked on, but instead, she allowed him to wrap his huge arms around her body and crush her to his chest, planting a wet sloppy kiss that got the attention of several of her audience.

Thank God you're here, Peter!

She licked the taste of him from her lips and closed her eyes, showing Brian the effect Peter's kiss had on her, and warmly accepted the feel of his fingers running down the cleft in her backside. It was something Brian would not be able to miss as well.

"Brian, this is Peter, my—"

"Boyfriend." Peter inserted before she could say otherwise. He extended his hand, and Abbey could tell the squeeze he delivered to Brian was uncommonly painful. "Nice to meet you, Brian."

Abbey thought Brian would have been discouraged, but to the contrary, the bitter expression on his face peeled away more of the mask and showed her more of his dark side. Or perhaps the darkness was growing.

"Likewise, Pete," Brian said in an obvious insult.

She would have explained something reasonable about Brian's visit if she had more respect for him, but she let him dangle, and he offered no explanation. Peter's fingers tickled her rear again, telling her he'd get it out of her later, most likely when she was naked if she was going to be stubborn about it. She stepped closer to him and rubbed her thigh against his, sending her left breast right into his bicep.

"Peter and his buddies are Navy SEALs, Brian," she said proudly and watched. If there was any impact at all, Brian expertly hid it.

T.J. and Tyler joined their little group. T.J. held a thin book, but all sets of eyes drilled into her ex.

"I'll take a raincheck on that dinner then," Brian said softly, trying to show how little an effect it had on him, and turned to leave.

Peter grabbed his arm before he could leave. "Not in your lifetime, meathead." He jerked his fingers from their grip on Brian's elbow. The grin that was returned was pure evil.

All four of them watched Brian turn the corner and leave the room.

"Who the hell was that?" asked Tyler.

"Someone who thinks he's more important than he is," answered T.J. as he craned his neck to make sure the newcomer was long gone.

"My ex-fiancé."

"Smart girl," said T.J. "He's dumb as a box of rocks, though, to let someone like you get away."

She was going to say something when the film came to an end.

"We can talk about it over dinner. It's show time now, boys!"

CHAPTER 5

T HE SEALS WERE introduced, as they had insisted, only by their first names. Even a couple of staffers from the Aquarium appeared at the back of the room to hear what they had to say. Abbey moved off to the side, while the three of them began their talk. It had been a stressful afternoon, capped by the insertion of Abbey's ex. Peter was on the lookout for the guy to show his face again.

He listened to T.J. show the *Navy SEALs for Wimpy Kids,* which was a combination coloring book and simplified story of how a wimpy kid could grow up to become a Navy SEAL. The autobiographical story was written by one of the amputees they'd been studying for pain treatment. As T.J. paged through all the pictures of running rubber boats over the rocky cliffs into the surf, lying on the "Midnight Sand," and staring at the moon while getting "Wet and Sandy," it brought forth a lot of fond memories from Peter's own training some three years ago. The audience of rapt faces scooted their chairs in a tight semicircle around the three of them, and before T.J. could finish going through the whole book, they were peppered with questions.

Peter noted the pages containing pictures of long guns and sidearms were especially of interest. Doing exercises and running with fifty pounds of rocks in the desert was not very popular. Peter chuckled to himself. He felt the same way. But he'd gotten through it, and that was all that counted.

Several times, he inserted stories of jumping out of airplanes at midnight and some of the places they'd visited, officially, of course. He winked at Abbey, who appeared distracted and was biting her lip.

Tyler and T.J. talked about spending time in the McKinley burn center in Texas. They all stressed the value of working hard, not for rewards and trophies, but so they could become the best version of themselves they could be. Peter added that there really was no failure in someone deciding the SEAL training wasn't for them, and that for many men, it was just a course to let a man know where his limits were, not necessarily a goal to achieve. Trying was being the hero.

And he'd had that conversation with many men who had washed out. He honestly felt it was true that

SEALs weren't better than anyone else. They were simply the ones who wouldn't quit.

By the time they'd finished a robust forty-five minutes of Q & A, the room was packed with as many adults as children. When a local news crew arrived, T.J. called it a wrap and refused to go on camera. Tyler and Peter backed him up one hundred percent. Some years ago, one of their ranks was targeted by a lone wolf terrorist who killed his teenage daughter in a suicide bomb attack. Real names and faces were always kept private, for obvious reasons. Nothing like finding your picture in the newspaper in a little village in one of the Eastern block countries where they weren't officially training. Worse, it had actually happened.

They received an enthusiastic round of applause and spent a few minutes afterward signing autographs in permanent marker on young scientists' forearms. Abbey kept the media at bay like a mother hen guarding her chicks. She also allowed the store manager to write down the name of the coloring book so young scientists in the future could pick up the paperback workbook in the "Friends of the Aquarium" section of the bookshelf.

It worried Peter every time he glanced over at Abbey, only to find her searching the crowd milling around the entrance to the large classroom. He needed to know what the story was there. He didn't like the little taste of this gentleman that lingered from the minute or so interaction. Men like him were the same the world over. In the face of innocence, they were emboldened to become mean. Peter not only didn't care for the gentleman, he didn't trust him one whit.

"Here you go," she said as she handed T.J. back his book.

"Thanks. I hope they help him out. He's got a lot of expenses we're trying to negotiate for him with the VA. Every little bit helps."

"I'll make sure our manager knows that as well." Abbey gave them a bright smile. "Thank you for today. And so sorry about the news crew."

"No worries," said T.J., batting the idea away with his hand. "Someone must have called them."

"Well, we only get news coverage when something bad happens here. Or when a celebrity comes." She wiggled her eyebrows and winked at Peter. "Not that you guys aren't celebs, of course."

"Of course," winked T.J. in return.

Peter wrapped his arm around her waist. "We're happy to give you guys a little publicity. Hope the crew found something else juicy to cover."

"Oh no. They were on their way out immediately when they found out they couldn't get your butts on their station."

"I didn't especially want my butt on T.V.," said Tyler.

Peter squeezed Abbey as she blushed at Tyler's re-mark.

"So you ready for some good home cooking? Nothing fancy, of course. I got some nice steaks. Just need a little time to whip up the chocolate cake." Abbey looked up at him, and he had to lean down and give her a lazy I-don't-care-who-sees-it kiss.

T.J. whistled. "You work fast, Watson," he said.

When Abbey came up for air, she was blushing, breathless, and her hair messed up because Peter had indulged in her silky softness. "That's the way I like it," she answered T.J.

T.J. AND TYLER followed behind them as Abbey drove him to her apartment.

"Don't expect anything too grand. I like simple cooking. I'm not a French chef."

Peter had been watching her profile and enjoying her pink cheeks and obvious bashfulness. "I like the simple things you do just fine. Haven't found anything yet I could ever complain about."

"Oh, I'm sure I have my moments."

"I doubt that." He wanted to ask her about the ex, but wondered if it was going to ruin their mood. He knew it was selfish, but a long lingering kiss before he had to share her with his other two buds might satisfy his need or inflame him for the rest of what he hoped would be another magical evening.

But that guy's hard expression really bothered Peter. Those kinds of men didn't go away or slink off into a corner somewhere. They took advantage of surprise. Not able to confront directly, they would take the tactical advantage of getting their prey when they were not paying attention. He knew how to handle that type. Only problem was here, in the good old US of A, he was limited in his quiver of options.

She didn't have a trace of worry on her forehead until he asked her what he had to ask her. He thought about it for a second and then launched his volley.

"So I want to know about this Brian guy. I'm coming from a place of not just caring about you, Abbey. I think he puts you in danger."

The familiar wrinkle he'd seen during their talk suddenly reappeared between her beautiful brows. She rocked her head from side to side and sucked in air, exhaling with her answer.

"I made a mistake, Peter." She gave him a quick glance then continued. "I thought he was a different person. In many ways, he is the exact opposite of what I saw, but for some reason, I admired his mannerisms, how he dealt with people, and how much people seemed to admire him."

"I don't hear anything in that about love, Abbey.

What about him did you see, really see?"

She frowned.

"Don't even go thinking I don't have a right to know. I'm trained to watch out for bad guys. This Brian fellow is a bad guy, Abbey. I'm not going to let you dismiss him so quickly."

"Oh, I dismissed him, all right."

"Not what I was meaning, honey. You can't underestimate a guy like that. I can see it in his eyes. He likes to hurt people. What I want to know is why you didn't see that."

They'd come to a stoplight. She slowly turned to face him. "Maybe I'm not trained to see that in people. Maybe I want to believe the good in people."

"I like that in you. But not when it puts you in harm's way, sweetheart."

He was as serious as he could be. He didn't smile, staring right back into her blue eyes, and kept the softness and tenderness away. It was important to him Abbey see the real danger there. If he was wrong, he'd ask for forgiveness later, but right now, he had to get her to see what he saw.

When her eyes teared up, he resisted the impulse to take her in his arms. That might just turn into something else. He needed to make sure his message was delivered. He couldn't help her with the confusion or the possible low-grade pain he'd caused.

A car behind them honked; the light had changed to green.

Abbey continued out into the intersection without checking traffic and nearly T-boned a late-crossing truck. She slammed on the brakes. Her face turned bright red, and she was shaking.

"Not your fault, Abbey. Let's get to your place. I distracted you, and I'm sorry for that."

She didn't look at him the rest of the way.

Barely two minutes later, they stopped into the parking lot of her complex. He raced around the car to open the door for her and pulled her up and into his arms. She was still shaking and had stiffened, but he held her until he could feel her melt.

"You did great, sweetheart. We'll talk about it later, okay?"

He pulled the hair from her face and held her between his palms.

"Okay?" he repeated.

She nodded and looked down.

He kissed her forehead. "Come on. Let's get something in our stomachs and satisfy these guys so they can leave us alone."

He felt her squeeze his waist back. "Thank you," she whispered.

Tyler and T.J. caught up to them as they were climbing the stairs. "Everything okay?" Tyler asked.

"Just a close call," answered Peter. "She's okay."

Abbey separated herself from Peter's grip, got out her keys, and unlocked her front door. "I'm fine," she said with defiance. "I wasn't paying attention." She gave them a sweet smile.

"Well, Peter does have that effect on women. Hang on, darlin'. Peter's an acquired taste," said Tyler. He got a punch in his arm from Peter, who made sure it was harder than necessary.

He helped Abbey in the kitchen, insisting the guys sit back and have a beer. She tasked him with stoking up the barbeque, which was something he excelled at. The deck outside had a couple lawn chairs, and T.J. and Tyler accompanied him for moral support.

They didn't say anything, but he knew that's why they were sitting down next to the barbeque. They were waiting for his answer to the unasked question. He'd applied the steaks and then grabbed his beer, leaning against the railing.

"Her ex is a piece of work. I'm seriously concerned for her safety, truth be told."

"I hear you," answered T.J. "Just asking a question, though. You sure it's your place?"

Peter knew he had the right to inquire. He wasn't sure what his answer was going to be, as he was formulating it while talking to them.

"One thing I know for sure is there are evil people

out there. Even if I didn't care for her, and, fellas, I'm falling hard here."

"Yup. Got that," said Tyler.

"Some things you just pick up on. She's in danger. I know she is. I can't let that go."

"I understand. But what can you do about it? We only got a couple of days here. Then we have to get back to San Diego. You can't go bringing her with us. I mean, you're not thinking that way, right?"

Peter could see T.J. was right.

"I'm thinking I might be able to discourage him somehow."

"That's not smart, Peter, and you know it," T.J. reminded him.

"You're probably right." He hated to admit it, but doing the smart thing wasn't what he was known for. Except he didn't want to hurt anyone else or to ruin his career. But somehow he had to get this guy out of Abbey's life.

"Does she have anyone here who can help out?"

"No family that I know of. But I really don't know."

Abbey brought out some chips. Both T.J. and Tyler stood up. Peter turned over the steaks without looking at her or showing what they'd been talking about.

"I'm just about done in here. As soon as the steak's done, we eat," she said and closed the sliding glass door behind her.

T.J. put his hand on Peter's shoulder. "Well, at least you got a little time to talk to her about it. Maybe it's not as much of a problem as you think, Peter. I'm hoping that's the case."

Peter peered out at the gardens and pool below. The sky was a deep rose color in sunset. He hoped he made the right decision. His heart was racing, just like before any good mission. He had confidence in what he could accomplish, if he had the right tools. The bigger question was, what was he going to need? And what was the outcome he desired?

He had to figure those two things out first. Then he could plan the course of action.

CHAPTER 6

ABBEY SAID HER good-byes to the two SEALs, standing arm and arm with Peter at the door, as if he lived there too.

"Not to worry, fellas. I'll make sure he's safe and sound in the morning."

"You do that," said T.J. "We got that place over in Peachtree City to visit tomorrow, and they're expecting us by ten. I can pick him up, say, eight or eight-thirty?"

"I don't work until Noon. Want me to fix breakfast?"

"You've done a lot already. Let's get this guy out of your hair, so I'll grab him at eight, and we'll get breakfast on the road. But I'll deliver him in one piece afterward. How's that?"

"I go from the Aquarium straight to Dante's. Deliver him over there, if you don't mind." She loved the little-boy-lost look Peter had on his face, his head whipping between the two of them.

Tyler shrugged. "Well, Peter, I'd say your day is pretty much all planned out. Lucky for you, your two social secretaries are in sync."

When the door closed, Abbey's palms sweated thinking about the "talk" she knew they were going to have when they were alone. Just as she suspected, Peter pulled her to him. Before he could say anything, she clasped her hands at the back of his neck, tiptoed to kiss him, and then pushed herself away.

"Let's get the kitchen cleaned up first. Then I promise we'll have that talk."

"Sounds good to me, honey."

She put on a jazz channel to ease her nerves, poured herself another glass of wine and gave Peter another long neck. The cleanup didn't take more than a few minutes. The dishwasher droned in the background as they took a seat facing her blank TV. She sat at one end of her couch, slipped off her shoes, and placed her feet in Peter's lap.

"You've known me, what, barely two days, and already I'm giving you foot rubs?" He grinned, but quickly pressed his fingers into places on her ankle and sole she hadn't known existed.

Abbey arched back and closed her eyes. It didn't take much imagination to fully comprehend what kind of a backrub he'd be able to give her.

"Oh. My. God. That feels divine, Peter."

"Good." He was focused on her feet unlike anyone in history had ever been. The devotion he showed her limbs was so extremely sexy. She had the urge to remove all her clothes and let him work over her entire body.

"So why don't you begin at the beginning? You said this guy was your ex. How did he show up here, or is this where he's from?" Peter asked.

"No. He's from California. I have no idea what he's doing here. Just showed up. I haven't spoken to him in over a year."

He nodded. "So what did he say?"

"He said it had taken him a long time to find me. Probably because I didn't exactly tell anyone except my future employer where I was going. But when I was finishing up school and we both lived in town, I never heard from him at first, never saw him except in passing, you know."

"Um hum. Where exactly was that?"

"Oh, sometimes they shopped at the same store. He found another girlfriend right away. In fact, I don't think he even saw me. His girlfriend did."

"Okay, where else?"

"I think I saw him in traffic a couple of times. Like I said, I'm sure he never saw me. He was always looking the other way, Peter. He didn't seem to want anything to do with me. At first."

"At first?"

Abbey stiffened, and she yanked her feet from Peter's tender hands, righting herself to sitting position a few feet from him on the couch. "One night, he was drunk. He stopped by the house right after my mother had died. Tried to pretend he was giving condolences, but he nearly—he tried to force himself on me."

Peter came to full attention. She watched as both his hands turned into tight fists. "Did he hurt you?"

"Scared me. I was right beside my purse, and after I kicked him in the groin, I sprayed him with pepper spray. I shoved him outside and called the police."

"Good for you. That ended it?"

"Oh yes. I never saw him after that. Not at all. Not in passing. Nowhere."

"Did you press charges?"

This was the part that was difficult for Abbey. Twisting her toe into the carpet, she answered him softly, "No." She'd been told by the police it was a mistake, but she was so convinced he'd not come anywhere near her she didn't want to cause the family more drama than they'd already experienced, especially with the fiasco with her dad. "Peter, I think he was drunk and I heard later he'd broken up with the girl he was seeing. Probably one of those somber moods he got into and needed some consoling and got angry when I couldn't give it to him."

"You were wise to trust your judgment."

"Well, he didn't get arrested, but there was a police report made. I did do that, but elected not to escalate it further. I told them I would if he ever bothered me again."

"And now he's here."

"Yes, but I think he has some other reason to be here."

"Abbey, that's not healthy." Peter slid over next to her and put his arm around her shoulder. "You don't know that. Don't make excuses for the guy. He dropped in unannounced and caught you off guard. That was intentional."

She squirmed under his arm and threw it off. "Don't be silly, Peter. There has to be an explanation."

"Probably, but maybe not the one you want to hear."

"Well, we didn't exactly give him any chance to do any talking, now did we?"

"Still making excuses for him. Abbey, you are such a smart lady. Think about this objectively. He *already showed* his true colors. If he almost hurt you once, he will do it again. You don't have to give him the benefit of doubt. That's your hang-up, and you've got to realize that. Unless…" Peter looked at his hands, rubbing them together, his elbows balanced on his knees.

"Unless what?"

"Unless you're wanting to let him be part of your life again."

He didn't touch her. She roared upright, not believing what she'd heard. It was outrageous, and it angered her.

"How could you say something like that? No. Never!"

Peter stood up and put his hands in his pockets at first, then crossed his arms and studied her expression. "So what's the hesitation? I don't understand, Abbey. Help me."

She inhaled and stared down at her feet again. What was she feeling? Regret? Did she miss Brian? Her heart shouted a resounding *no* to that question. What was it?

With the pounding in her chest as background noise, the clouds lifted and she saw clearly what had happened the instant she'd recognized Brian. She didn't know if he would believe her, but it was the truth, and the truth Peter deserved to hear.

"Peter, I didn't want to make him angry. I wanted him to go away."

"You are afraid of him, aren't you?"

It was difficult to tell him, but Peter already knew what she was feeling.

"I think so."

He was in front of her in an instant, kneeling, holding their entangled hands on her thighs. "Abbey, trust me. You're right. You're totally right to be afraid of him. You should never ever again be alone with him. Do you believe me, honey?"

She read in his sincere eyes that he cared about her. But then, she'd thought the same thing about Brian at first. "I know you're right, Peter. I wish I wasn't so cowardly."

"No. You're just super trusting. Like I said before, that's a great quality and something I admire in you. You see the good in people, or think you do. But some people, by their actions, cannot be trusted. He knows all the right things to say, but his actions speak volumes. Stay away from him."

"Not like I can stop him," she whispered.

Peter's forehead became more lined, the edges of his mouth drooped, and he squinted. He scrambled to his feet and paced across the room in front of her. When he finally stopped, he put his hands on his hips and stared down at her. "No, but I can. That's what I'm afraid of."

"No. You shouldn't get involved."

"But I already am involved, Abbey. Can't you see that?"

Of course it was what she wanted to hear, but it was also caused him some distress.

"When I go back to San Diego, you'll be all alone here, and that worries me. I'll be too far away to do anything should you need me."

She knew she should feel more afraid, but seeing Peter standing in front of her, totally focused on protecting her and focusing on her safety, thrilled her. She knew he couldn't help but be her protector. It was carved into his DNA. No matter how much she'd try to convince him otherwise, he wouldn't be persuaded.

She rose to her feet slowly and stepped timidly toward his hulking form. His shoulders were broad, his arms solid steel and corded with veins. He even had muscles in his jaw, his neck, and other places that made her blush. This big man had a heart as big as his massive body.

She could try to object, of course. But what good would that do? Abbey knew he would not change his mind. And it wasn't what she wanted anyway.

No, the only thing she wanted to do right now was submit to him. Be everything she could be to him to thank him for caring. And maybe, just maybe it would be enough to hold them loosely together until she could figure out a way to visit him in San Diego. It was something to think about in the days and weeks to come.

Right now, all she wanted was to have him wrap his arms around her and kiss her senseless.

"I'm sorry, Peter. You're right. No one's cared about me and my safety like you have." She slipped her fingers up his chest, traveling over the bumps his nipples made under the cotton shirt up to the thick bands at his neck, one hand tracing to press three fingers against his lips. "I tell myself I can be responsible for everything. But there are some things I cannot do alone. It's scary to need you so much, Peter. I hope—" she admitted as she moved up on tiptoes and lightly kissed his mouth beneath her fingers—"you'll forgive me. It's all new to me."

His arms wrapped around her waist, smashing her lower body against his groin. She rolled her head back and he kissed that sweet spot she loved, just below her ear and under her chin. She felt the vibration in his chest as he moaned at her taste.

"Let's not think about this any longer tonight. We can always talk about it tomorrow, maybe tomorrow night. We have time. Not very much time, but I don't want to waste it talking about my ex. Make love to me, Peter. I need that more than ever."

He picked her up, one arm under her knees, and effortlessly carried her to the bedroom. Gently laying her on the bed, he and removed his shirt, watching her. She began to take off her blouse, but he stopped her.

"No. My job," he reminded as he unbuttoned her and kissed her flesh underneath, pulling up her bra and teasing her knotted nipples with his tongue and his teeth. "This is my job, Abbey, and I take it seriously."

His fingers were thick and slightly clumsy, but the scars on his hands felt delicious against her tender flesh. He adjusted his button fly jeans so they slipped off his slim hips. Next, he unzipped her pants, peeling them off her thighs and depositing them in a pile on the floor. That fully revealed her white lace thong panties, with her bra pushed up over her breasts and the shirt open wide. He pulled her panties down just far enough so he could get access to her waiting sex.

At last they were one again. There would be no talk about all the things they *should* talk about. As he rode her, he loved all the tension and worry from her body. He left her pliable and sweaty. Her heart loved him with a fever that burned every cell in her body.

The only thing left for her to do was to show him how much she needed him, without worrying if she was holding on too tight. That would be a concern and thought for another day. But not tonight.

Tonight was made for love.

CHAPTER 7

PETER AWAKENED BEFORE Abbey did, watching her sleep. The sky began to turn a robin's egg blue, but was stubborn about it. Birds to chirped on the railing of her balcony, twittering in quick staccato conversations. All seemed right with the world, except something black loomed in the background.

He recalled their conversation last night, confirming the fear she finally acknowledged she'd been masking. He knew all about that. He was a master of it himself. All the guys had to mask things they were afraid of. It had nothing to do with looking more competent or manly—it was a requirement that he be able to focus and partition things off, shield some of his emotions from his decision-making. That was the real trick: learning to shield just enough, never too much. Emotions gave him that gut reaction he'd need in a firefight or a dangerous wartime situation. Not having them made him a liability not only to himself, but his

Teammates.

He was lucky that he had the Brotherhood. Those guys would die for him. It was probably hard for the general public to understand. He also felt lucky that he'd been allowed to participate on the Teams. Lucky that at such a young age he'd found something so exciting and compelling to live his life for.

But now there was Abbey, and this was a different kind of fear. He didn't want to go overboard, get all Commando with her life. Heck, maybe she didn't really want that. Maybe she wasn't ready. But it would be hard to step away.

Should he?

He examined not only the beautiful evening they'd had, but also the way he felt giving the talk to the youngsters at the Aquarium, how proud he'd been of his job and his brothers. He looked inside his heart and saw the women and children and old men he'd saved in Afghanistan, Yemen and North Africa. He pictured those he could not save. He knew a big chunk of that portion of the world didn't have the luxury of doing what they wanted to do. They lived in survival mode. Part of his mission was to help bring about a peace for them by ridding their population of the idiots who were enslaving them, the evil people who cannibalized their religion and made everyone's life hell. Even the unwittingly incompetent assistance from his own country and others he'd seen there. It was a jigsaw puzzle with a million pieces thrown in the dusty sand.

But here, he could walk away. Except that wasn't what he was about. He had to do the one thing that would be the most difficult for him; he needed to assess what Abbey wanted. What she *really* wanted. Not what she *thought* she wanted. If he got any indication she was just sleepwalking through the night with his heart, then he'd have to get out quickly, even if his hunch was correct. Maybe set something up with Dante. Dante would know a resource here in Atlanta to give her aid if he couldn't be the one.

She stirred in his arms, twisted her silky body against his, and shocked his libido into full speed ahead, but he was going to hold back. Her hair was all over the place, even partially covering his face, which was so odd for him, because normally he didn't like anything obstructing his view or tickling his cheeks. She smelled like a woman in lust, remnants of her perfume still lingering on the sheets as she moved. Her body was like a furnace, and it got hotter and damper between her legs as she hugged his upper thigh between hers. The delicate lips of her sex pressed against him.

Yes, he was a lucky man. But today he'd have to do the real man-thing—the right thing. He'd never forgive himself if he didn't. He would always feel like he'd cheapened any chance they had to be together.

Brushing the hair from her face, he palmed her cheek as delicately as he could. His hands were paws with claws or something, disfigured and scarred from cuts and broken fingers and calluses he wore as the badges of his trade. They were like the tats on his upper arms, his back, and the one encircling his ankle made of thorns.

"Sweetheart, are you awake?" he whispered to her ear, then kissed her there.

A smile appeared on her lips and she nodded, with her eyes still closed.

"Abbey, we need to get up. I have to be ready soon, and I want a chance to talk first, remember?"

Her warm blue eyes dazzled him as she shined her bright face like a spotlight into his soul. God, he was going to miss her!

She stared at his lips, covering them with her fingers like she'd done so many times recently. "These lips did so much damage last night, Peter. What you do with your tongue, what you do with your kisses. No wonder they call you a lethal killing machine, my—"

Abbey had stumbled over the word. He knew what it was. It was what he wanted to call her as well. She was his love already. He was certain of it. But it could not be spoken yet. He saw she held back, too.

He drew her up on top of him. She lowered her

mouth to his and gave him a proper good morning kiss, while his fingers traced down her back, over her smooth butt cheeks, and down her thighs to her knees. She shivered under his touch. Her thigh pressed against his hardness.

Fuck it.

He wrapped his arms around her and threw her back against the mattress, clutching her hips and pulling her onto his length. He watched her arch and receive him with that satisfied smile that just drove him wild.

"God, Abbey, what am I doing?"

She kissed his ear and then whispered, "You're fucking me good morning, sweetheart. You're my breakfast and lunch until you can come back here and be my dinner." She giggled before quickly turning serious and groaning. Pulling him deep inside, she spread her knees and clutched his buttocks.

He'd wanted to wake up earlier and take his time with her, if she was willing, but he needed the sleep. Today was going to be an emotional one as they interviewed several ladies who had knowledge of the human smuggling with the Garcia gang. But he needed to come back home to this woman in this bed first. He needed to start the day out right. He needed to rock her world, however short the encounter would be.

As they later peeled themselves from each other,

their sweat merging deliciously between their bodies, he was still out of breath as he pressed her warm body against his and held her as tight as he could.

She gave him a whimsical look. "Peter, I can't breathe!" she whispered, embellishing it with a croak in her voice.

"Sorry! I'm so sorry," he said as he unfurled his arms and gave her space. "I just—"

"No, Peter, it's perfect. I have never felt so—"

There was that hesitation again as she stumbled over that word he'd yet to utter to her. Although he wanted to do so, it was unfair until after they'd talked. She saw his thoughts, he knew she did. In that moment, the understanding of their feelings for each other were both delivered and received. She trusted him fully.

Which was why it was so difficult to get up out of bed. "Come on. Take a shower with me, okay?"

She groaned as he pulled her arm and then hoisted her body over his shoulder and carried her into the shower. She screamed at the cold water on her ass. He let her slide deliciously down his body, their chests together as the now-warm water sluiced between them.

He purposely didn't act on all the little impulses he had as he helped her shampoo her hair, washing all the evidence of last night's love-making off her silky flesh. When she did the same for him he stood perfectly still, his arms dangling at his sides, letting her wash wherever she wanted to and touch any part of him she needed to. In every respect he knew he belonged to her. Peter had never before felt this way about anyone.

She put on a white fluffy robe, wrapping her hair in a towel, while he dried off and dressed. He watched her make coffee and sat down on the couch, going over in his head all the things they had to discuss.

The steaming mug wasn't as hot as her body was under that white robe and as she sat down next to him and presented his coffee, his other hand found its way through the opening to squeeze her left breast.

She set her mug down, pulled the robe off her shoulders, and sat with her full breasts and knotted nipples fully exposed to him.

He whistled, but didn't touch. "Dayum, Abbey. This is no way to have a meeting."

"Oh yes, it is. This will help us keep everything in perspective."

"I like that perspective, Abbey, but you're making it hard to concentrate."

She smirked, angled her head, and pulled her robe back up and over her shoulders, wrapping it across her chest, completely covering up.

"Better?"

He was sorry he'd said anything. But he was running out of time. He set his coffee mug down on the table. "Come here, Abbey."

She was only too glad to climb into his lap. Her finger traced the arch of his ear. He pulled the towel from her head, threw it to the side, then laced his fingers through the back of her head, and pulled her hungry mouth to his. "This is about us, Abbey. This is about keeping this alive," he said as he kissed her, teased her tongue with his, and searched her face. "This isn't about the chemistry we have or the beautiful sex. This is about making sure we have many, many more days and nights like this."

She stopped her toying and rubbed her thumbs over his lips again. "Tell me again."

"This is about us," he repeated as her fingers touched him.

"Yes. I want more of us," her whisper answered him. As she gazed into his eyes, he felt she'd pulled his heart right out of his chest.

He stopped massaging her ass, which was positioned on his thighs, allowing his groin to feel the warmth between her legs. Placing his hands safely on her shoulders, he decided he'd not try to sit down at a table or next to her on the couch. He'd keep her this way, dangerous as it was.

"So here's the thing, Abbey. I can't let anything happen to you. I say this to you not as someone who has—" Now it was his turn to stumble. He decided to just come out with it. "Someone who has formed attachments—" He couldn't find the right words and he balled one hand into a fist. She grabbed that fist from her shoulder and held it to her cheek until he uncoiled it and laid his fingers against her. She kissed his palm, and then pushed it between her thighs.

Now he knew he couldn't do it this way. He withdrew his hand. "I asked you just a few moments ago what I was doing."

She nodded, her eyes dancing, toying with him.

"You answered me correctly. But it's not the whole truth about this attachment between us. This is special, Abbey. This is something I don't want to end."

"Me neither."

"So help me out here. Let me get some things off my chest."

"Okay."

"I've never been married. I've had girlfriends, of course, but no one has affected me like you have. I knew it the first time I saw you."

"Under water. In a wet suit."

"Exactly."

"Your species sort of thing. Biology?" She wrinkled her nose and furrowed her eyebrows.

"*Not* biology."

She gave him a mock frown.

"Well, yes, some biology, of course. But it comes

from here." He placed her palm against his heart. "I mean this with utter sincerity; I couldn't live with myself if anything ever happened to you, Abbey. I'm quick to make decisions, I know, but something about this feels so right."

Her gaze was serious. "I feel the same way, Peter."

"Good. That's a great start."

Her puzzled expression showed up again.

"Being a SEAL, we're gone a lot. We do stuff we can't talk about. Sometimes I come home from deployment and I'm in a rotten mood for a month or two afterwards. I am jittery and a real asshole sometimes. We work it out with each other, other guys on the teams. Some guys don't have that reaction or hide it better. It's hell on the girls—and the families."

"So what are you saying?"

"As good as it feels right now, it might not always be this way, and I want to warn you. I have this radar for bad guys. I feel sometimes like I'm a magnet to them. I see them everywhere. That can be a problem. But it's me, and it's my problem. I get territorial, and I won't let anything interfere with those I—I love."

There, he'd said it.

She put her fingers to her own lips, and her eyes filled with tears.

"I'm sorry. Did I say something wrong?"

"No, sweetheart," she answered through her tears.

"It's all good. Trust me, it's all good."

"I don't want to candy-coat it or lie to you. I'm a piece of work. You hook up with me and you're in for a wild ride, Abbey. I'm not very flexible."

"I think you're flexible. You were flexible last night—" she teased with tears streaming down her cheeks.

"That's a whole different thing. I'm going to be demanding. I'm going to insist on certain things from you. I need to know if you have the strength to tackle all those things. And, believe me, you have no idea how difficult it might get sometimes."

"Why are you giving me all this doom and gloom?"

"Good. I'm glad you see it that way. Like I said, I don't want to sugarcoat it."

"So what is it you are telling me that you don't want to just come right out and say?"

"I want you to go to the police and make a report on Brian. I want you to take precautions in dealing with him. I want you to tell Dante and the other people at the Aquarium that he's not to be anywhere near you. You need to put everyone on notice about you. No more Mr. Niceguy treatment with him. Can you do that, sweetheart?"

"Are you sure?"

"Abbey, I told you some things would be difficult. Even if I'm wrong, this is the safest thing I can insist you do. If I could, honey, I'd take you back to California with me."

Her eyes blinked, wicking away the tears that had formed.

"This is way too soon to be talking about all this, but I wouldn't forgive myself if I didn't ask you to do this. Will you? You can't back down with what I'm asking. There is no easier or gentler way. You have to trust me. Do you?"

"Yes."

He was relieved and exhaled the breath he'd been holding. He placed his hands behind her head and pulled her to him again and just before they kissed, he whispered, "It's because I love you, Abbey. Do this for me, sweetheart."

The long kiss was more than a prelude to sex. He could feel her happiness. He could also sense how nervous she was, and that was a good thing. He was usually one hundred percent accurate about people's character, and what he saw of hers confirmed he'd been right again. And he knew she should be scared. Being with him, committing to him, if they could get there by some miracle, was going to be the most dangerous thing she'd ever done or would ever do.

But, if she let him, he'd protect her until the day he died. Nothing was going to harm her ever again. No one was even going to get close.

CHAPTER 8

S HE KEPT SNEAKING little looks at him as if discovering a chink in the armor or something that indicated he'd not been honest. The truth he'd told her, from his heart, was the most beautiful thing she'd ever heard. The warning he gave her only made her love him more. He made no excuses for being a possessive, fierce lover, the best friend anyone could ever want, and someone she could always count on.

The question in her own mind was whether she had what it took to keep up with him? He'd walk away if she asked him to. He'd stay and shower her world with love. But she had to take that step and do what he'd asked. She had to do it consciously and not by accident or pure chance.

All that remained behind them. From today onward it would be fully intentional. This bond between them was real, after all—love of the highest order. The crazy thing was that she barely knew him. And it didn't matter.

He caught her in one of those looks. "Is there something wrong?"

"No. I'm just wondering what lucky star I was born under."

"My star. You were born under my star. So I could take care of you. It was all predestined. You had no choice in the matter!" He smiled, softening what was a strong comment that made her heart race.

She missed him already as T.J. and Tyler appeared at her door.

"Here you go, lover boy, since I doubt Abbey has anything that would come close to fitting you." T.J. shoved a fresh pair of red, white, and blue boxers at Peter's face. "Go change, but make it quick."

"Now you've given me an idea," said Abbey. "I'd actually like to see what something lacy would look like on him."

Tyler piped up. "Don't try it Abbey. He'd be so pissed."

"I'd be pissed at what?" asked Peter as he returned from the bathroom.

"Here, I'll make sure you have these fresh and cleaned when you get home tonight, Peter."

"That's a serious sign. Already doing laundry for you, sport." T.J. winked at her. She liked the big medic and was glad Peter had such handsome and upstanding men to serve with. They looked her in the eyes without flinching or diverting their gaze. They answered questions directly, even when they were joking with her. They seemed to accept life on life's terms. They didn't preach and didn't seem to judge the fact that Abbey and Peter had formed such a quick, intense bond.

That's probably the way they all do it.

Peter took her in his arms. "You remember what you promised. Don't delay. Get your butt down to the station, and then make sure everyone at both workplaces has the card of the officer you talk to, okay? You make it easy on them, just in case."

"I will. Thank you, Peter."

They kissed and he gave her a light spank on her rear. She waved at T.J. and Tyler and heard T.J. grumble on the way down the stairs, "Shit, Watson, we gotta get you some Red Bull or a gallon of coffee so we can wipe that pussy-whipped look from your face."

Tyler added a big, "Oh Yeah!" to that.

"I'm fine."

"Oh, I got that, but hell if I'm gonna let you shoot a gun or drive a car. I've seen a lot of guys fall, but man, you've got it worse than anybody I've ever seen." He went on making more comments, trying to convince Peter of his opinions, but they'd traveled out of earshot.

She watched them climb into their rented Hummer and waved at him from her balcony. He didn't look back.

Inside, Abbey dressed, gathered her lady pirate outfit for Dante's, packed her makeup and wash kit, and threw in her expensive bottle of perfume she didn't often waste on the clientele at Dante's. But, tonight, she would see Peter again. She wanted every meeting, re-introduction to him to be a showstopper.

She put her hair up in clips, including one she'd brought back from Hawaii that had imitation red flowers attached to the teeth. She was careful not to apply too much makeup so she didn't give the police the wrong impression.

She checked her cell for messages and the time and then clicked it silent, placing it in her purse. She wore navy blue leather tennis shoes with white laces. She checked her jeans and long-sleeved knit top, threw on a red windbreaker, hung her purse over her shoulder, and headed out into the hallway.

The odd scent of alcohol and too much aftershave mixed with body sweat hit her. And not the kind of sweat she'd been enjoying all morning.

Brian's stubble and blotchy red skin highlighted the dangerous wildness of his bloodshot eyes. He looked angry and in so much pain, she nearly felt sorry for him.

Until he pushed her hard by the shoulders and shoved her backward onto her living room floor. He slammed the door behind him.

She moved away from him, doing a reverse crab-like walk while reaching for her purse that contained the pepper spray.

Brian was quick to grab the purse away from her fingers.

The kick to her stomach shocked her. She curled up into a ball, gagging at the pain and trying to get her breath. A sharp pinch and burn at the side of her neck warned her too late of the danger. What had he injected her with? Immediately, her eyes grew lazy but she fought to keep them open.

Peter had been so right about Brian being dangerous, and how she hadn't taken him seriously enough before. She'd been drugged, perhaps was going to die from an overdose of whatever he put into her system. Was he trying to control her or kill her?

But she didn't have time for these unhelpful thoughts. She had to remain strong. As the blackness seeped into her vision, she knew she'd fight him off, if it was the last thing in the world she ever did. Right now, it was the only thing that mattered.

CHAPTER 9

THE CUTLER HOME for Girls was on a quiet street of well-manicured lawns. Peachtree City was known for licensing golf carts to travel down the main roads, and a series of pathways were created that crisscrossed neighborhoods all throughout the quaint little town. Some claimed there were more golf carts than cars here. It was also said that it had more golf courses per capita than any other city in Georgia. That was saying something when it seemed like the whole state was completely nuts about golf.

Peter didn't much care for the serenity here, and he knew that, as a group, the SEALs would attract way too much attention if they ever wanted to party. It just wasn't his kind of digs.

Tyler was impressed with the sizes of the houses. Row after row of large semi-mansions with picket fences and raised beds of flowers were everywhere, lying under lacy fifty-year-old trees that provided a gentile shade. "My mom would enjoy coming here. She'd love to paint all this color."

T.J. nodded and scanned the lovely gardens as he checked the address he clutched in his fingers. "I'm guessing they hardly need a neighborhood watch program. Use a different kind of toothpaste and you'd get arrested."

Peter chuckled. "That's exactly what I was thinking."

"But the golf would be nice, right, Peter?"

"Amen to that, brother," he answered.

"So how did they get a halfway house for girls here in this town?" Tyler asked.

"Beats me. But man, those girls are probably thinking they've died and gone to Heaven. This has got to be one of the safest places I've ever seen." T.J. shook his head.

He compared numbers to the sheet of paper and announced, "We're here."

They parked against the rounded curb and slowly walked the flowered path to the front door.

A tiny brass plaque was placed discretely above the doorbell, *Cutler House, est. 2010.*

Just as T.J. was about to push the button, they all heard a sound that was completely foreign to the neighborhood. The unmistakable chatter of children's voices and laughter came from the backyard, along with splashing water from a swimming pool.

He rang the bell, and quickly there appeared a white-haired woman dressed in pants and a big work shirt with a brightly colored apron covering.

"Can I help you?" she asked.

"We're the guys from the Navy here to talk to one of your girls about—"

"Oh yes! You're the Navy SEALs. I honestly expected you closer to ten o'clock. You're early."

"Yes, ma'am." T.J. agreed. "We just thought we'd give as much time as possible."

"Very well. Listen, you boys take a seat at the kitchen table, and I'll go get Elaina. Mrs. Foster will get you some cookies and tea or coffee, if you like." She motioned toward the kitchen area, closer to the sounds of the backyard noise. "And, by the way, I'm Mrs. Cutler."

T.J. shook her hand first. Then Tyler and Peter followed suit.

"Thank you, ma'am, for allowing us to come," said Peter.

"Nonsense. Any way we can help out, we're here to do it. As you know, we don't live in a perfect world, gentlemen."

"Roger that, ma'am," mumbled T.J.

They entered a large kitchen with a huge wooden table in the center that must have been able to seat twenty people. Another elderly woman in a flowered apron turned and gave them a warm smile. The kitchen smelled like fresh cookies. Peter had rarely seen anything so perfectly idyllic. It was every little kid's dream of a perfect grandmother's home, reminding him of his elderly relatives in Tennessee.

"I'm Doris Foster. Now you boys sit down here and let me fix you up. You want coffee, tea, water? I also have some sweet tea, our specialty here."

"Sweet tea sounds nice," T.J. said. Both Tyler and Peter agreed.

A large china plate was placed in front of them, and piled high with about twenty warm chocolate chip cookies. "Help yourselves," she said as she placed a small saucer in front of each of them. She returned later with a tray containing three tall glasses of sweet tea, garnished with a sprig of mint.

A very pregnant, dark-haired, Indian-looking young woman in a white smock, entered the kitchen, her head bowed. Mrs. Cutler had her palms on the young girl's shoulders.

"Gentlemen, this is Elaina. Her English is not very strong, but she does indeed have a story to tell." She pulled a chair out next to Peter. "Have a seat, Elaina. These are the men I told you about. No reason to be afraid of them. They're here to help you find your little sister."

Peter glanced between T.J. and Tyler, and he could

see in T.J.'s expression complete surprise.

The girl began to cry silent tears, which she brushed away with the backs of her hands.

"Ah, Elaina. I'm so sorry," cooed Mrs. Cutler. "You want me to get Maria to translate for you?"

"Yes, please, Mrs. Cutler," Elaina said in a weak voice. She chanced a quick peek at Peter and what he saw there melted his heart. "I'm so sorry. My English—" She shrugged, indicating this was perhaps all she could do.

"Thank you for telling us your story," Peter said. "We're here to do anything we can do to help."

Elaina looked blankly between the three men, while Mrs. Foster brought her a glass of ice water.

"I don't think she understands you, Peter," said T.J.

A heavyset girl with long black hair braided like a crown atop her head came bounding into the room. She was older and much more outgoing. She stopped near each of the SEALs, bowing slightly and shaking their hands one-by-one. She took a chair next to Elaina.

After she put her hands on her shoulders, she said, "This is Elaina. She wants to tell you that she was kidnapped at the age of ten and sold to a family in Sinaloa who were looking for a house maid." She said something to Elaina, who responded back in Spanish and nodded. "But she soon became the plaything of the master of the household, and then his sons. She is fifteen now and this is the baby she made with the master or one of his sons."

Peter felt his hands tighten into fists. T.J. had buried his forehead in his hands, elbows on the table.

Elaina spoke to Maria, and again Maria translated. "About two years later, they needed another servant so these men paid for someone to go kidnap Elaina's little sister from her village."

Maria waited for Elaina to say something more. "She says to tell you it was the worst day of her life, seeing her sister being carried—" Maria and Elaina bantered back and forth a bit. "Like she was sleeping?"

"Unconscious?" T.J. asked her.

"Yes, yes, that is the word. Unconscious. But she was not dead, just drugged, sleeping, you know?"

They all knew too well what that meant.

"For nearly two years, she was allowed to stay with her sister in the same room, unless the Master wanted Elaina for sex. He threatened that he would have sex instead with her little sister if Elaina didn't agree, so she did." Maria listened to Elaina say something very emotional and cover her face with her hands. Maria put her arms around her and tried to console her.

The three SEALs didn't know what to do.

Maria continued, still holding the sobbing Elaina. "They took her womanhood. Now she will never have a proper husband. They passed her around between the three of them like she was a pet. I would spit, but Mrs. Cutler has a clean house. These men are devils, and they should all be put to sleep."

Peter couldn't agree more.

"She doesn't have to tell me the rest, because I've heard her story many times. We've met several other girls who come through here, all pregnant, some of them too sick to have the babies. Mrs. Cutler tries to help them find good families to live with or churches to help sponsor them. And she's agreed to help with the childcare when they work. Many of them work here in the golf courses, in the kitchens, the housekeeping staff. Mrs. Cutler is very nice to all of us. No one has to leave if they don't want to."

"Sounds like Mrs. Cutler is a saint," mumbled T.J.

"That she is, son," added Mrs. Foster. "Anyone want a refill?" Maria held up Elaina's empty glass.

Just then, Mrs. Cutler entered the room, holding a fussy toddler. "Doris, can you go change him please while I sit with our guests?"

"Sure." She took the squealing child and disappeared into one of the rooms downstairs.

Mrs. Cutler sat at the head of the table. "Have you told her whole story yet, Maria?"

"Not quite. I haven't told them about Lupe being sold to the man from Baja."

That got all the SEAL's attention.

"Was this a Mr. Garcia? Did you see him or hear of his name being spoken?" T.J. asked.

Elaina nodded meekly, recognizing the name.

Mrs. Cutler interrupted, "That's the name they all come back with. Santiago Garcia. As long as I live, I shall never forget that name," she added. "About the third time I heard it, I called my Congressman and had him over for tea. I attempt to stay under the radar here, trying not to draw too much attention to what we're doing. But this was something I just couldn't take any longer. It sounds like this man is a monster."

"Ma'am. I'm not supposed to tell you this, so you can't say you heard it from us, but we helped put his brother in the ground a few months ago. And this Santiago guy is the one we're after now. God willing, we'll be your spear, Ma'am," said T.J.

"God has nothing to do with it. I put my faith in him daily," said Mrs. Cutler firmly. "But as far as a spear? I put my faith in you Navy SEALs first. I think I can be forgiven for that little indiscretion."

Peter liked the woman immediately, and he could see everyone else did too.

T.J. had been right. She was a saint.

CHAPTER 10

ABBEY WOKE UP in a motel utility suite with a kitchenette and dining table. Zip ties dug into her wrists and ankles. He'd tied a rag across her mouth, which she thought she might be able to dislodge, if she worked at it. She was lying sideways on a bed, secured with a bicycle cable to the metal headboard. She pulled to see how secure it was and found it would cut into her wrists if she pulled too hard. Worse, it made quite a bit of noise, as the headboard banged against the wall.

Her stomach was swollen and bruising, her headache pounded to hard, it made her ears buzz. But as the moments passed, she became more and more alert, gaining in strength. This was heartening.

Throwing her legs over the edge of the bed, seeing if perhaps she could stand, she found she could. But, with her ankles cinched so tightly, her balance was precarious. She sat back on the mattress, extending her legs in front of her, using the headboard to rest against.

Her feet were slightly swollen, because the ties had been pulled in haste and done too tight.

She tried to maneuver her gag by rubbing her mouth against her shoulder, then attempting to hook her thumb under the fabric to pull it up over her nose, but the cotton was too stiff. Spitting into the material, getting the whole area in front of her mouth sopping wet, she nearly had the thing off when she heard a key work the door lock. Seconds later, she came face to face with Brian.

He was carrying packages of groceries. She recognized the recycled plastic tote bags she had from the same grocery store.

"Ah, you're awake. Are you hungry?"

He'd shaved at least, and he appeared to have cleaned up a little from before, but he still had that wild look in his eyes. He was playing some alternate reality game with himself, acting as if she was a willing guest and he was going to entertain her with food and good cheer. In fact, she knew he had something else on his mind.

But as long as he didn't hurt her, she'd bide her time, play along and wait for the right opportunity to do something.

He set the groceries down, and put a six-pack of beer in the refrigerator, along with some eggs, orange juice and other food stuffs wrapped in white paper.

He'd stocked up for a few days, she noted, with the cans of soup and a box of cold cereal with almond milk. He remembered she liked almond milk on her raisin flakes.

"You ready to eat yet?" he repeated his question.

She drew her fists up to her mouth, indicating she couldn't talk.

"Yes, well, we're going to have to use sign language, Abbey. I'm afraid I cannot trust you. Not yet."

She made the mental note he had the confidence he could convince her he wasn't the enemy. There was absolutely no chance of that. That must mean she was close enough for someone to hear her scream.

All of a sudden, nausea washed over her. At first, she thought it was the reaction to whatever he'd put in her veins, but as her stomach lurched and tried to expel its contents, the pain in her belly exacerbated. She remembered the kick he'd delivered, which had knocked her out of breath and landed her sprawling on the floor.

Then panic took over as the bile exploded all around her gag, even driving some up her nose. For a minute, she worried she might suffocate, so she tried to moan and then rocked wildly against the bedframe causing the walls to rattle.

He loomed over her, watching her deal with the disgusting vomit dripping down her neck and chest.

She drilled him a look that told him her opinion of him.

"Abbey, I'm sorry I have to do this. If you'll promise to be good, I can clean you up, but if you pull anything, I'm afraid I'll have to restrain you further. We have so much to discuss. Decisions to make, sweetheart."

He leaned over to brush the hair from her forehead, and she yanked her body away from him, trying to send her legs to the other side of the bed. She rubbed the wet gag around her mouth on her shoulders again to get rid of some of the bile, but at last she gave up. Leaning forward and bowing her head, she cried as privately as she could.

She didn't know if he intended to just scare her, hurt her badly, or kill her. The man in the room with her was as much a stranger as ever. The internal incriminations she felt as she swore at her lack of judgment and her naïve devotion to this man in her past didn't help. She was furious with herself.

But she remembered how Peter had talked to her about staying away from Brian, had talked to her about his wanting the element of surprise. If only she could get to her cell phone or her pepper spray, hopefully both tucked into her purse she saw thrown into a side chair, the contents beginning to spill out.

Brian left and returned with a cool towel and began

to wipe the vomit from her cheeks, her chin, her neck, and then finally down to her upper chest. His other hand lingered on her right breast, and he squeezed, his dazed eyes seeking some kind of erotic response from her which she was quick to not show. She narrowed her eyes and attempted to turn away from him, but he held her shoulder in place while he continued to wipe her face, her forehead, and then dabbed her forearms clean.

Her hair had bunched up into a ratted mess at the back of her neck. She wanted a shower, but didn't dare suggest it. She considered asking to go potty, where she might have some privacy, or better yet, be able to lock herself in the bathroom. She deduced that if there was a kitchen, there would probably be a large sharp knife, which might be the method of self-defense, perhaps something that could untie her wrists.

"Are you comfortable? You warm enough?"

She allowed him to experience the awkwardness of his one-way conversation. If he did ungag her, she'd scream as loud as she could without a moment's hesitation. And that's probably why he wouldn't free her.

"You want a blanket? I've gotten your blouse wet. Maybe I should remove it and you can get warm under the extra blanket? Yes?"

She glared back at him without indicating she

wanted anything.

"Well," he said as he rose and took the towel to the bathroom, to rinse off, "time to make us a little light lunch. I have cream of tomato soup. Your favorite, as I recall."

She wished he hadn't been so observant of her likes and dislikes. She'd burned all memories of him and his tastes from her brain. Now she could see he'd never really let go.

She wondered how he was going to feed her if he wouldn't remove the gag, but she stowed that thought away and averted her eyes down.

Brian angled his head and dried his hands on his pants. "I'll be back in a little bit, sweetheart. And then we can share a nice meal."

Immediately, she began working the gag with her thumbs and finally slipped it down over her chin, resting on her collarbone.

She inhaled and screamed, "Help! Somebody please help me! Help!"

Brian was on her in an instant, his hand covering her mouth as he leered at her, smashing his nose against hers until it hurt. "I don't want to hurt you, Abbey, so don't make me. If I do, it will be *your* fault. We haven't had that talk."

His eyes were red with a ring all around his eyelids. His scent was sickly, mixed with nervous sweat. She'd not noticed the twitch in his left side, or how his lip involuntarily quivered and his left eye squinted. But distressing her most of all was the total lack of concern for her. Instead, he acted like she was the instigator of his problems, that she caused his discomfort and pain. There was no doubt in her mind that he did experience pain. At some point, it would become too much to bear and he'd act out.

He hurriedly yanked the gag up over her nose and mouth, which drove her into a panic that she would not be able to breathe. He ran to the kitchen, brought back a roll of duct tape and cut a wide swath off the roll, quickly affixing it to her mouth and cheeks after removing the gag. But at least her nostrils were not covered.

He pointed the scissors at her mouth, and she stared in horror at him, thinking he was going to stab her there.

"Stop squirming," he whispered tersely. He gripped her chin, puckering her mouth, and angled the scissors at the little seam between her lips. Pressing hard, he snipped. She jumped as the sharp blade caught a tiny piece of her upper lip. Several drops of blood oozed from the hole he'd created in the duct tape. The warm liquid dropped to her chest.

The scissors in his right hand, his left hand contorted her face, hurting her. For a second, she thought perhaps he was going to stab her in the chest or poke out her eye. Terror escaped in a whimper; tears streamed down her cheeks. She shook, knocking the bedframe against the wall, refusing to be quiet.

"Stop it or I'll slit your throat," he said as he held the open blade of the scissors under her chin and let her feel the coolness of the metal resting there. "Don't test me, Abbey."

She knew she was on borrowed time. She was out of options. He pressed the blade against her throat, and she could feel it begin to slice into her flesh. "If you don't stop squirming, I will do it. Don't make me, Abbey."

His wild eyes spoke of his desperation. The tears that filled her eyes were not for herself. They mourned the loss of the wonderful love she shared with Peter, the pain of knowing that they would never be able to be together because of this man. This man had the power to take away her happily ever after. If she could just get the scissors in one hand, she'd find a way to kill him. She might die also in the struggle, but she wanted to end him so he wouldn't prey on anyone else.

He abruptly stood, cursing down at her. Her shaking continued, tears mixing with the blood coming from the shallow wound on her neck and upper lip. She couldn't stop crying.

He threw the scissors into the kitchen and disappeared, returning with another syringe filled with light yellow fluid. She whimpered as he jammed it in her neck and dropped the plunger, his face a mere inch from hers. His sneer loomed as she tried to breathe through the effects of total blackness.

Am I dying? Peter, am I dying? Will you catch him for me and put him away in a cage? Better yet, remove him from the face of the earth. Can you do that for me, Peter? I'm—sorry I couldn't fix you breakfast this morning.

Everything went dark.

CHAPTER 11

T HE THREE SEALs exchanged phone numbers with Mrs. Cutler, also giving her the number to the joint task force at Coronado that would lead to their handler, Sr. Chief Petty Officer Collins. Wherever in the world they were sent, the Sr. Chief would know how to reach them.

"You call us if someone else shows up or if you hear anything else about the Garcia gang, okay?" T.J. asked her.

"No problem," said Mrs. Cutler. "I'm going to dance a jig when this cretin is put behind bars or joins his brother in Hell."

Peter was surprised such frank language came from such a sweet older lady. He was fascinated with her warrior spirit.

"Can I ask you why you do this? You could just enjoy your retirement. This is a wonderful town to live in. Why get involved in all this with the girls?"

"Who would do it then? You think the government could do what we do? It's not that they don't want to; they can't. They don't know how."

"But why do you care, aside from simply being a wonderful person?" he pressed.

They had walked to the front door. T.J. and Tyler were already out on the porch when Mrs. Cutler stopped, put her hand on Peter's forearm. "Because I lost a granddaughter a few years ago. She was in Mexico during spring break, traveling with a couple of her girlfriends. They got separated from her chaperone, one of the mothers who went along, and although the authorities found her two friends, shaken up but otherwise unharmed, they never found my granddaughter."

"How long ago was this?" Peter asked. T.J. and Tyler listened quietly.

Mrs. Cutler pointed to the brass plaque above the doorbell. "April of 2010. I vowed that I'd do what I could. We tried for six months, her parents and my husband and myself. They divorced over it. My husband died of a heart attack."

Peter embraced her, not sure if it was the correct thing to do, but he found this wiry older woman's strength impressive. When he released her, he expected to see tears in her eyes, but they were dry. "I'm still here, and I'm not going to rest until we find the people who did this to my granddaughter. I must bring her home, regardless of her condition. She will stay with me here in Peachtree City. If she needs it, she can have the plot next to my husband. But she must come home."

"Mrs. Cutler, do you have a picture of your granddaughter?" asked T.J.

She slipped around the corner and they heard a drawer open. She returned with a school photograph of a petite, attractive brown-eyed girl wearing a cap and gown. "It was her Senior year. She never graduated with the rest of her class. She never wore these in earnest. It's the most recent picture I have of her." She hesitated for a second and then extended her arm, holding it out to T.J. "It's yours."

"Thank you, ma'am."

T.J. and Tyler hugged her as well. Peter gave her one more just before they parted.

Back in the truck, Peter tried to breathe deeply to calm his nerves. He was so angry that such a woman would have to endure so much pain it was clouding his senses.

Tyler and T.J. said nothing. Everyone sat alone with their private thoughts.

"I'd like to call Abbey. Would you guys mind?" Peter asked after some time had passed.

"Knock yourself out," answered T.J.

"God, I miss my kids," Tyler whispered to T.J.

"No kidding. First thing I'm going to do when we get home? Hug them. I always remember after I'm away, always realize I don't do it enough. None of us ever do, right?"

"You're right about that. I can't wait to see them," whispered Tyler.

Peter had dialed Abbey's number but got her voice message, so he left her one. He figured she was cavorting with the shark and angelfish in the big aquarium tank.

"Hey, Abbey. We're all done here in Peachtree. Heading back to Atlanta. It's been an intense few hours. I'll tell you about it when I see you. We should be back in about half an hour, so will see you at Dante's. If there's a change in plans, give me a call. Miss you, babe."

He was struck with how fragile life was and vowed he'd not take anything for granted.

They stopped for an afternoon snack at a barbeque shack near the freeway. The place was packed with locals stopping by to pick up to go orders. The clientele was varied, from men in business suits to mothers with kids. Some college age couples stopped by, and a local amateur baseball team, still in their dirt-smeared uniforms invaded the place and took up the only seating. T.J. directed Tyler and Peter to a picnic bench outside a gas station next door. They devoured the ribs and slaw as if it had been a week since they'd eaten. T.J. did not join Tyler and Peter in sharing a beer but instead crushed ice with his mineral water.

T.J. wiped clean his fingers with the alcohol wipes the kitchen had provided with their order. He carefully brought the picture of the Cutler granddaughter out, laid it on the table, and spoke down to it.

"Well, Miss Chrissy Cutler. You have a mighty fine grandmother. We're gonna see what we can do about bringing you home, sweetheart."

"Amen to that," said Tyler. Peter nodded his agreement.

Peter's phone rang, and he answered without checking where it came from, he was so sure it was Abbey.

"Hey, sweetheart!"

The gruff voice on the other end of the phone was Dante's. "Been a few months since my wife's called me that, but never you mind. This isn't a fun call, Peter."

He sat straighter and watched as T.J. and Tyler perked up, watching him carefully. "It's Dante," he whispered to his teammates, putting his hand over the microphone on his cell.

"What's up, Dante?"

"I got a call from the Aquarium. Abbey didn't show up for work today, and they wanted to know if they'd gotten her schedule mixed up and she was instead at the restaurant. I told them I hadn't seen her all day. You know where she's at Peter? In about a half hour, she's going to be late here too."

Ice water coursed through Peter's veins.

"No fuckin' clue. No one's seen her, then?"

"No, sir. Can you stop by her apartment. Are you close?"

"Yeah. We're about twenty minutes away. We'll go there and give you an update. Has anyone heard from her today at all?

"Nope. She didn't call to say she was sick, or going to be late, or anything. I don't have to tell you I'm worried. This isn't like Abbey at all. Not at all."

Dante signed off and Peter stood. "Come on. Abbey's missing. She hasn't shown up at the Aquarium today for work and Dante hasn't seen her, either. We gotta go by her place and check to see if she's okay."

ABBEY'S CAR WAS missing. Had she had an accident somewhere and was stuck in her car, waiting for help? Peter toyed with several scenarios before he allowed himself the final, most dreaded one. Was her ex involved? Part of him realized it was entirely possible.

They stopped by the manager's office and he said he hadn't seen Abbey all day. He offered to open her apartment door to help check on her, but wouldn't let them have a key. All four of them jogged down the hallway on the second floor until they came to Abbey's apartment door.

At first, nothing appeared out of place. But upon

closer inspection, Peter saw a few drops of what smelled like vomit on the rug in the living room. The bed had been made. Everything in the kitchen was clean. But the carpet near the liquid was lined with several ruts in the carpet tufting. The table nearby the easy chair was at an odd angle, and the lamp was not centered on it, like Peter had seen before.

"Someone's fallen here," he said to T.J., pointing out the sharp furrows in the carpeting. "The lamp's been bumped, and the table moved."

The manager stood meekly in the doorway, his hands in his pockets. T.J. spoke to him.

"You sure you didn't see her leave?" he asked.

"No, sir. Let me get back down to my unit, and I'll ask the gardener and the pool man, okay?" He left as soon as T.J. nodded.

Peter called Dante. "Something's wrong. Her car's missing. But it looks like a struggle happened here, like someone fell or knocked a few things out of place."

"I'm on speed dial with the Chief. I served with his pappy, the biggest toughest SEAL I ever met, Mr. Franklin Hicks. You want me to have him get someone out there?"

"I'm thinking, yes. But if she's missing and not in an accident somewhere, I have a good idea who's responsible. You seen anything of her ex, Brian?" Peter asked.

"Nope. As far as I know there hasn't been anyone hanging around lately even before you guys. I'll ask a couple of her friends, though."

"You should call her again, Peter," said T.J., placing his hand on his shoulder.

His fingers shook, but he redialed her number. Once again, he got her voice message.

"Abbey, sweetheart. We're getting a little worried now. Please call me back. We've got the Aquarium people and Dante asking us where you are. Are you okay? Try to get a call back. Love you."

Both T.J. and Tyler's heads whipped up to attention.

Chief Turner Hicks showed up in person. If his father was one of the biggest, toughest badass SEALs in the history of the SEALs, his son was times two. The guy filled the doorway like it was midnight. He brought along two of his deputies and a homicide detective, though there was no evidence of murder. Based on Dante's description of the encounter Peter had with Brian, he could tell their radar was on high alert.

They asked questions, taking pictures of the room, and had all of the SEALs submit their prints to rule out in case they decided to formally treat the apartment as a crime scene.

But when the manager showed up with the landscaper and one of his helpers, Peter's worry doubled.

"He was helping her up, like she was sick, you know?" the workman said. "Her head was rolling around, and I couldn't tell, but it didn't look like she was walking on her own at all. He put her in the passenger seat, strapped her in, and then took off down that way." The helper pointed to the right.

His description matched Brian's. Peter was frustrated because he couldn't look Brian up. He didn't have his last name. Abbey had never told him the name of the winery she was going to be working for, either.

Then Dante called back. "You're not going to believe this, son. One of my girls said she had a LoJack installed on her car before she left California. The police can send a signal and turn it on. If she's not too far away, we might be able to find it."

It only took twenty minutes to hear back from the police scanners that one of their uniforms had run across the signal and had located the car parked at a hotel near the freeway west.

It was only a five-minute drive from her apartment. The Chief asked the SEALs to stand down. They promised they'd not interfere, but would not be prevented from following behind them.

Less than an hour after Peter had gotten the initial call from Dante, Peter, T.J., and Tyler gathered around Abbey's red car in the parking lot at the Suite Sixteen motel and suites.

One of the deputies brought the motel manager with him.

"They're in room 301."

CHAPTER 12

ABBEY AWOKE WITH the bright afternoon light scorching her face. She felt horrible and gagged, but soon realized the duct tape across her mouth could pose a problem. She swallowed heavily and closed her aching eyes. Stirring behind her on the bed alarmed her. Someone's hand snaked across her waist, splayed at her sore stomach, and pulled her upper torso back toward his body, resting spoon-like next to her on the bed.

Brian!

The thought of him holding on to her—not only kidnapping her, but physically touching her—nearly made her retch again. She groaned and tried to worm her body away from his. Her ankles remained tightly secured.

The hand swept her forehead and hair from behind.

"No worries, sweetheart. If you could just find it in

your heart to understand me. All I want is to talk to you. To explain what's going on here."

Abbey knew exactly what was going on. She was the victim, yet Brian wanted understanding and care. The hypocrisy was too rich for her to stomach, and she involuntarily dry-heaved again. Her head was bursting in pain like something inside was going to explode. It wasn't lost on her that the reason for the duct tape was twofold. He wanted to shut her up, and he had no interest in whatever she had to say.

The man had no capacity to care about anyone but himself.

"You hungry yet? You didn't have the soup I prepared for you. Let me go warm it up."

She felt the delicious coolness at her back as his sweaty body left the bed and allowed her a few seconds of peace. She heard some voices outside the window and down below, and for a second, she thought perhaps she heard T.J. or Peter, but she couldn't be sure. The air conditioner suddenly kicked in, the drone wiping out all other sounds. She sighed and closed her eyes again because the bright light stung them. Dehydration likely added to the soreness in her eyes. If she could play her cards right, maybe she could get some liquid. But not too much. She was grateful she didn't have the urge to go potty and all the dangers that that could pose.

Her mind wandered over the events that had led up to this moment. She relived the pain as Brian kicked her, forced her on the ground, and then injected her with some drug, twice. She saw his eyes, heard the rattle in his voice, and smelled his pungent body odor. And then she thought of Peter.

Images of them holding hands, the way he smiled and joked with his buddies over dinner, the talk he gave to the kids at the Aquarium, the whispers they shared in bed as they explored the wonder of their perfect mating flooded back. Her heart filled with sadness until she understood that at least she'd had these memories, and however long Brian would let her live, she'd not give up on those. She'd fight, somehow, to get them all back again.

If only I could get hold of the pepper spray or my cell.

She arched up, her wrists remaining bound, still secured with the bicycle cable attached to the headboard. On her elbow she propped herself up high enough to see the contents of her purse strewn on the seat of the chair in the corner. She saw the red corner of her phone cover, and the black canister that held the spray. If she could get loose somehow, she could execute a repeat defense. She sunk back down to the mattress, feeling weak.

Brian returned behind her and sat on the bed, placing something on the nightstand. "I've brought some nice warm soup so you can have some. Would you like this, Abbey?"

She did want something in her stomach and hoped that meant he'd remove the tape, so she turned her head and looked up at him over her shoulder. Her heart sank.

In his right hand, he held a small white bowl, but out of the top of the bowl was a straw. On the nightstand was a glass of water, also with a straw in it. Her chances of getting the tape removed vanished, triggering another wave of sickness.

She rolled back toward the window, closed her eyes, and forced herself to think positive thoughts. But her spirits were sagging. Unless she could reason with Brian, she had no chance to crack his thick shell of whatever was driving him. She had to continue to hope that somehow she could get through to him. It would be a total mistake to just simply up.

She adjusted her hips, and scooted towards the headboard, attempting to sit up. Brian set the soup down, came over to the other side and helped prop her up, holding her under her armpits. As she sat, still immobile, she noticed Brian glancing around the room. He brought the chair with her purse on it over next to the bed. She stared at how close that purse was and how easy it might be to grab the contents when he returned, brushed everything to the floor, and held the soup on his knees before extending it in her direction. The straw was aiming for her mouth. She saw steam coming from the bowl and, briefly worried that it would be too hot to drink.

Too hot to drink.

Too hot to drink.

His sickly sweet smile nearly ended her composure. He was focused on getting the straw to the opening he'd cut with the scissors, pulling aside a small section of tape and wiping off crusty blood. In slow motion, the hot liquid came closer and closer to her. She leaned forward, as if cooperating with him, her wrists still bound, sore and red, and lying to the right of her thigh. Abbey waited for what she hoped would be the right moment, reveling in the steam, trusting it would be hot enough to throw him off so she could get to her purse.

She inhaled as the straw was inserted into the opening in the tape. Then she pushed up with both fists, aiming at the bowl. The contents flew right into Brian's face.

He screamed and stood up, wiping hot soup from his face. Pulling back her knees, she kicked him in the groin with both feet, sending him sprawling on the floor.

Her feet made contact with the ground, attempting to scoop her purse contents up alongside the length of the bed. She was desperate to reach the pepper spray, but couldn't get it close enough to be able to grab it. Brian saw what she was attempting. He raised his fist to strike her when the door burst open. Two men dressed in black, weapons aimed at Brian's chest, barged in and shouted for him to remain standing in place.

Brian lowered his arm but was admonished to raise both his hands over his head in a command so loud it shook the windows. As the two rescuers barked orders, tears started streaming down Abbey's cheeks.

Brian was tossed to the ground on his belly, his hands yanked behind his back and secured with thick black zip ties. The second man approached, asking, "You okay?"

She nodded, making it obvious she couldn't talk.

"It's gonna hurt for a second. Ready?"

She nodded again. He quickly ripped the tape from her face, and although the searing pain was nearly more than she could handle, she took in a deep breath of freedom for the first time.

Her rescuer grabbed the pillow next to her and wiped away blood flowing from the now-re-opened cut on her lip.

"Did he hurt you anywhere else?"

She held her hands up and shook her head. "No," she tried to shout into the pillow. He pulled it away and continued to use a corner, dabbing her wound. He cut the ties on both her wrists and ankles and she was finally free.

She leaned over, stretching to touch her toes, and then felt the dull ache in her stomach. She inhaled and pulled up her bloody shirt, showing him her belly, which had begun to turn brownish blue. "He kicked me. It hurts here," she said as she pointed to the right side of her rib cage.

"You were lucky, ma'am. Anything else? Did he sexually assault you?"

"No, thank God."

The room shook as she heard pounding like horses hooves. Peter was at the doorway, his face panic-stricken. She thought to herself she must look a fright, her hair all messed out of place, blood covering her shirt. But in a flash, he was at her side. He picked her up despite the objection of the man in black and held her in his lap as he sat on the edge of the bed. He was squeezing her so tight again, she couldn't breathe. She hit his shoulders like she'd done before, pushing herself away from him.

"Peter, I can't breathe!"

His eyes watered, but the relief on his face was like being embraced by everything she loved about home, everything she loved about everything. The best part of it was he was there to protect her, and she knew he would never leave.

CHAPTER 13

PETER ACCOMPANIED ABBEY to the hospital in the ambulance and wouldn't allow the paramedics to exclude him. The tussle was going nowhere when Chief Hicks separated them.

"Would you two school kids quit this? We've got a patient to get to the Emergency Room!" He directed his considerable three hundred pound countenance on the skinny medic who looked barely out of high school. "You tell me what kind of smart is it to go arguing with this Navy SEAL and his lady!"

"But, Chief, the rules—"

"Fuck the rules, son. This man is a lethal killing machine. He can kill you with his little finger. You best remember that next time you choose to get in his way, you hear?"

"Yessir." The medic mumbled and allowed Peter to assist him getting Abbey's gurney into the van. Once inside, Peter turned and thanked him.

"Thanks, man. But you laid it on a little thick, don't you think?" he whispered to the Chief.

"My daddy would have my ass if I did it any other way. Now you stop holding up progress here and get your butt down to Emory. I got a whole pile of paperwork, and I *hate* paperwork, so you best get yourself as far away from me as possible. I'm gonna be chained to the desk for the next several hours, and then I gots an appointment with my wife. You get my drift?"

"Indeed I do, sir. Well, I better let you to it, then."

"Don't go lettin' that little one explore the outside world too much for the next few days. She needs to stay right by your side, you hear?"

"Yessir. I couldn't agree more. Thanks again."

"All right then." He slammed the door shut.

Peter barely had time to slide closer to Abbey before the ambulance lurched, the sirens blared, and they were off for the emergency room. He tried to keep out of the paramedic's way, but he found the tech irritating with how he mumbled his instructions like it was the first time he'd done it. He didn't share the results of her blood pressure, and Peter decided not to bug him further.

Abbey's smile looked like it came straight out of a horror film. Her swollen lip was bright red and caked with blood that clotted up into her nostril. Another dried streak ran down her throat. Since the first chance he had to hold her hand, she clutched his like she was never letting go.

Her tears glistened in full sheets at the sides of her face, and he could see were collecting in her ears. This caused the paramedic to ask her if she was in pain.

"No," she whispered with her puckered lopsided lip as she stared only at Peter.

"So any sharp pains at all anywhere?"

"Just this," she said as she lifted her shirt.

Peter looked at the pink, blue, and brownish bruises that were forming on her stomach and the dark purple bruise that surely indicated a broken rib on her right. Before he could ask, she explained what happened.

"He kicked me."

The attendant gently stroked over her skin with his hand gloved in blue latex, pressing gently and asking for places it might hurt.

"It all hurts, but not like this," she said as she pointed to the rib area.

"Brian wouldn't be in one piece if I'd seen that," Peter said.

"You were right, Peter."

"About what?"

"Element of surprise. He kicked me to knock me over to avoid getting kneed again. I opened the door and he was on me."

"But he didn't—"

"No. He didn't touch me that way."

Peter stood, trying to balance in the rolling vehicle, leaned over, and put his cheek against hers. She kissed his ear. He slid his fingers beneath her head and squeezed her hair, whispering to her, "God, I love you."

She tried to angle her shoulders up to press herself against his chest, whispering, "I thought I lost you. I thought I'd never see you again." She groaned and fell back. The paramedic gently pulled Peter away.

"Not a chance, sweetheart. Never leaving you out of my sight again, if I can help it."

Of course it was ridiculous to say. He'd have to go on deployments. She'd be left behind on plenty of occasions. But it made him feel better to tell her that anyway. She knew what he meant.

The hospital buzzed with activity. It took nearly three hours before all the tests, including a urinalysis could be completed. The sample was turned over to the police as evidence. It was determined the drug he'd used was short-acting and would not be something she'd have much residual effect from, an animal tranquilizer, she was told. The police also mentioned that because she bled it would upgrade Brian's likely charges. And he'd used scissors, considered a weapon. The drugging and kidnapping was the most serious of charges, but there had been evidence of stalking and a host of other things. They were reassured that Brian's chance for bail, due to his apparent mental state, was next to nil.

She was not wrapped for the confirmed broken rib, but given instructions on its care. At last, Peter was able to wheel her out to T.J.'s rental Hummer. All three SEALs lifted her up and placed her carefully in the second seat, strapping her in. Tyler returned the wheelchair. Peter sat next to Abbey, held her hand and kissed her palm as they headed back to her apartment.

"Did they find my purse?" she asked.

"Yup," Tyler held up a blue hospital bag. "Your wallet and cell phone are here, too."

"Oh great. Can I call work?"

"Honey, Dante already knows you won't be in for awhile. I didn't know who to call at the Aquarium."

Abbey made a very brief call to the store manager, assuring her she was not hurt.

"She said the news crews were back. This time they were getting a story we liked. Interviewed half the staff," she said after she hung up.

"You got any ice, Tyler?" Peter asked.

"Sure do." He slapped a white packet he retrieved from the hospital bag and handed it to Peter.

He pressed it gently against her side. Abbey hissed in pain. "Sorry, but it's good for you. Am I pressing too hard?"

"No, it's just cold!"

"Hey, Tyler, got another one?"

"T.J., I think we better get some more of these after we drop them off, what do you think?"

"Good idea," agreed T.J.

Peter held the pack out in front and Abbey turned in his direction, presenting her face. Before he placed the cold pack against her, he gently kissed her. "Welcome back, sweetheart," he whispered.

Tyler and T.J. lead the way and brought her things in while Peter held Abbey across his chest. Once inside, he gently laid her down on the bed, sat next to her and held her hand, kissing her knuckles and palm.

"Look, we're gonna go get a few things you'll need. They give you a prescription to fill?" T.J. asked.

"Yes, but I don't want anything for pain. Thanks, though."

"You want some some soup?"

Her eyes got the size of golf balls.

"Absolutely not!"

T.J. GAVE THEM the news that Kyle had ordered them all to return to San Diego on Monday. Their next deployment had been stepped up. Peter knew that meant they had no time at all, and he couldn't even ask to be relieved of this rotation or be late with the planning and workup.

After discussing their options, Peter made the suggestion to call Mrs. Cutler and see if one of her ladies would be willing to come help Abbey out for a few days. The woman was only too pleased to help out and promised to be there herself on Monday.

"You guys can stay here. No reason to leave," Abbey said to T.J. and Tyler.

"Nah, give you guys time alone. But thanks. We'll pick you up early. If there's anything else you need, Text me," said T.J. "Our plane doesn't come until three, but that gives enough time to get Mrs. Cutler set up."

When the door closed behind them, Peter was finally alone with Abbey.

"They didn't listen. Brought some clam chowder and it smells wonderful. I'll bet you haven't eaten anything all day," Peter said.

She finally agreed.

He balanced two bowls and brought in the small loaf of French bread, placing it on a napkin between them. He was going to feed her the soup, and she took it from him.

"I'm not an invalid," she said rather pointedly.

"Just trying to help out."

"I have other plans for you." Her eyelids were half-closed as she peered over the spoon and sipped the warm soup.

"I'm taking that as a very good sign you'll fully recover." Peter's voice had suddenly dropped, husky with need.

"I'm halfway there right now," she responded.

The soup was finished, and Peter removed their dishes. "Shower?"

"Let's talk first." Abbey was insistent.

Peter removed his shoes and climbed up on the bed next to her, propped by the pillows against the wall. He took her hand in his and massaged the length of her fingers, smoothing over every joint of every finger and pressing against certain points in her wrist, the back of her hand, and up the inner side of her forearm. He could feel her becoming pliable and soft, and losing resistance to his touch as her pain subsided.

"That feel better?"

"Divine!"

He picked her hand up and stared down at her palm. "I have to leave tomorrow, but there's no way I'm leaving you behind. I want you to come to San Diego as soon as you can."

"How long before you leave?"

"Maybe a month. Normally, it's a couple of months, but this time, we're in a hurry, and we've been there before."

"You going where?"

"Mexico. Baja."

"Okay. And how long will you be gone?"

"A month, probably less."

He sucked in air. She stroked his cheek with her fingers. "Thank you."

"For what? You owe that to the police, to Dante."

"No, for being you, Peter. For walking into my life and changing everything about it."

He stared into her teary eyes, leaned over and kissed her carefully. Her sour expression when they separated told him her lip still hurt. "So I guess I'll have to use my lips somewhere else, then." He pretended not to notice her sly grin. Coming to his knees, he lifted her shirt over her head, and removed her bra, mindful of her rib. He suckled one of her nipples.

"That feels better already."

"It tastes wonderful. Dessert for me."

Her fingers sifted through the back of his head as he gave attention to her other nipple. Coming up for air, she framed his face with her palms.

"I thought it was all over today. I thought I would never have this again."

"Impossible, Abbey. This was destined from the very first time I saw you in that skin-tight blue and yellow dive suit. I knew it then, and I know it now. You belong to me, Abbey. And I'm completely yours."

Her eyes welled up again. "I'm the happiest girl alive, Peter." She traced his lips with her fingers.

"So San Diego… You're coming with me."

"Yessir."

He liked that she didn't push him further. "But I have one more condition, Abbey. You didn't get to keep your promise to me earlier, but this one is non-negotiable."

He could see she was braced for something.

"Marry me."

"I've known you, what, three days?"

"I think two and a half."

"Is that enough time?"

"You know what I think. I've already asked myself that question, and I've answered it. Marry me, Abbey. I want you to come home to. I don't want you outside our community. I want you safe, with us, close by all my best buds and the wives. If you get to San Diego and you don't like it, well, okay." He was going to continue but she placed her fingers over his mouth again.

"My answer is yes, Peter. Sounds like you don't want a long engagement."

"I'm not really that way. Why string it out and make me suffer?"

She smiled. "Good. Glad that's settled. Now, stop talking and get me naked," she whispered.

Peter helped her to her feet, removing the rest of her clothing, and then walked her to the bathroom. At the mirror, she gasped, getting finally a good glimpse of her face and swollen features, as well as the bruising on her midriff. He watched her accept it, and then turn into the shower.

He was so frantic to get his jeans off him he got his foot stuck. Finally naked, he helped her shampoo her hair, smoothing down the soapy bubbles over her silky skin. He drew her backside to his chest and held her as tight as he dared, kissing the side of her neck. Under the steamy shower he took a position on the tiled bench seat, lifted her by the hips and pulled her against him. She bent her knees at his thighs, moved up and down on the length of his shaft, undulating carefully, presenting her breasts to his mouth.

Without urgency, he made love to her, allowing her to guide him, holding her, kissing her bruised parts, and smoothing over her bumps and ridges, all the dark and exciting places of her body.

She was the perfect compliment to his hardness. She was soft where he was firm. Her moans and passion inflamed him to give her everything he had.

She'd thanked him for coming into her life and making everything different. The real truth was that this golden mermaid had given him the life he'd dared to dream possible.

And for that, he'd protect and cherish her forever.

This is not the end. It is only the beginning. You will be reading more about Peter and Abbey's journey soon.

You know you gotta have more SEAL stories! You can order the next book in Sharon's Bone Frog Brotherhood series, SEALed At The Altar.

For a better deal, order one of the following SEAL Brotherhood Bundles, featuring some of the characters in this novella:

Ultimate SEAL Collection, Vol. 1
(four full length books and two novellas)

Ultimate SEAL Collection, Vol 2
(three full length novels)

ABOUT THE AUTHOR

 NYT and USA Today best-selling author Sharon Hamilton's award-winning Navy SEAL Brotherhood series have been a fan favorite from the day the first one was released. They've earned her the coveted Amazon author ranking of #1 in Romantic Suspense, Military Romance and Contemporary Romance categories, as well as in Gothic Romance for her Vampires of Tuscany and Guardian Angels. Her characters follow a sometimes rocky road to redemption through passion and true love.

Now that he's out of the Navy, Sharon can share with her readers that her son spent a decade as a Navy SEAL, and he's the inspiration for her books.

Her Golden Vampires of Tuscany are not like any vamps you've read about before, since they don't go to ground and can walk around in the full light of the sun.

Her Guardian Angels struggle with the human charges they are sent to save, often escaping their vanilla world of Heaven for the brief human one. You won't find any of these beings in any Sunday school class.

She lives in Sonoma County, California with her husband and her Doberman, Tucker. A lifelong organic gardener, when she's not writing, she's getting *verra verra* dirty in the mud, or wandering Farmers Markets looking for new Heirloom varieties of vegetables and flowers. She and her husband plan to cure their wanderlust (or make it worse) by traveling in their Diesel Class A Pusher, Romance Rider. Starting with this book, all her writing will be done on the road.

She loves hearing from her fans:
Sharonhamilton2001@gmail.com

Her website is:
sharonhamiltonauthor.com

Find out more about Sharon, her upcoming releases, appearances and news from her newsletter, **AND receive a free book** when you sign up for Sharon's newsletter.

Facebook:
facebook.com/SharonHamiltonAuthor

Twitter:
twitter.com/sharonlhamilton

Pinterest:
pinterest.com/AuthorSharonH

Google Plus:
plus.google.com/u/1/+SharonHamiltonAuthor/posts

BookBub:
bookbub.com/authors/sharon-hamilton

Youtube:

youtube.com/channel/UCDInkxXFpXp_4Vnq08ZxMBQ

Soundcloud:

soundcloud.com/sharon-hamilton-1

Sharon Hamilton's Rockin' Romance Readers:

facebook.com/groups/sealteamromance

Sharon Hamilton's Goodreads Group:

goodreads.com/group/show/199125-sharon-hamilton-readers-group

Visit Sharon's Online Store:

sharon-hamilton-author.myshopify.com

Join Sharon's Review Teams:

eBook Reviews:

sharonhamiltonassistant@gmail.com

Audio Reviews:

sharonhamiltonassistant@gmail.com

Life is one fool thing after another.

Love is two fool things after each other.

REVIEWS

PRAISE FOR THE
GOLDEN VAMPIRES OF TUSCANY SERIES

"Well to say the least I was thoroughly surprise. I have read many Vampire books, from Ann Rice to Kym Grosso and few other Authors, so yes I do like Vampires, not the super scary ones from the old days, but the new ones are far more interesting far more human then one can remember. I found Honeymoon Bite a totally engrossing book, I was not able to put it down, page after page I found delight, love, understanding, well that is until the bad bad Vamp started being really bad. But seeing someone love another person so much that they would do anything to protect them, well that had me going, then well there was more and for a while I thought it was the end of a beautiful love story that spanned not only time but, spanned Italy and California. Won't divulge how it ended, but I did shed a few tears after screaming but Sharon Hamilton did not let me down, she took me on amazing trip that I loved, look forward to reading another Vampire book of hers."

"An excellent paranormal romance that was exciting,

romantic, entertaining and very satisfying to read. It had me anticipating what would happen next many times over, so much so I could not put it down and even finished it up in a day. The vampires in this book were different from your average vampire, but I enjoy different variations and changes to the same old stuff. It made for a more unpredictable read and more adventurous to explore! Vampire lovers, any paranormal readers and even those who love the romance genre will enjoy Honeymoon Bite."

"This is the first non-Seal book of this author's I have read and I loved it. There is a cast-like hierarchy in this vampire community with humans at the very bottom and Golden vampires at the top. Lionel is a dark vampire who are servants of the Goldens. Phoebe is a Golden who has not decided if she will remain human or accept the turning to become a vampire. Either way she and Lionel can never be together since it is forbidden.

I enjoyed this story and I am looking forward to the next installment."

"A hauntingly romantic read. Old love lost and new love found. Family, heart, intrigue and vampires. Grabbed my attention and couldn't put down. Would definitely recommend."

PRAISE FOR THE
SEAL BROTHERHOOD SERIES

"Fans of Navy SEAL romance, I found a new author to feed your addiction. Finely written and loaded delicious with moments, Sharon Hamilton's storytelling satisfies like a thick bar of chocolate." —Marliss Melton, bestselling author of the *Team Twelve* Navy SEALs series

"Sharon Hamilton does an EXCELLENT job of fitting all the characters into a brotherhood of SEALS that may not be real but sure makes you feel that you have entered the circle and security of their world. The stories intertwine with each book before...and each book after and THAT is what makes Sharon Hamilton's SEAL Brotherhood Series so very interesting. You won't want to put down ANY of her books and they will keep you reading into the night when you should be sleeping. Start with this book...and you will not want to stop until you've read the whole series and then...you will be waiting for Sharon to write the next one." (5 Star Review)

"Kyle and Christy explode all over the pages in this first book, *[Accidental SEAL]*, in a whole new series of SEALs. If the twist and turns don't get your heart jumping, then maybe the suspense will. This is a must read for those that are looking for love and adventure with a little sloppy love thrown in for good measure." (5 Star Review)

PRAISE FOR THE
BAD BOYS OF SEAL TEAM 3 SERIES

"I love reading this series! Once you start these books, you can hardly put them down. The mix of romance and suspense keeps you turning the pages one right after another! Can't wait until the next book!" (5 Star Review)

"I love all of Sharon's Seal books, but *[SEAL's Code]* may just be her best to date. Danny and Luci's journey is filled with a wonderful insight into the Native American life. It is a love story that will fill you with warmth and contentment. You will enjoy Danny's journey to become a SEAL and his reasons for it. Good job Sharon!" (5 Star Review)

PRAISE FOR THE
BAND OF BACHELORS SERIES

"*[Lucas]* was the first book in the Band of Bachelors series and it was a phenomenal start. I loved how we got to see the other SEALs we all love and we got a look at Lucas and Marcy. They had an instant attraction, and their love was very intense. This book had it all, suspense, steamy romance, humor, everything you want in a riveting, outstanding read. I can't wait to read the next book in this series." (5 Star Review)

PRAISE FOR THE
TRUE BLUE SEALS SERIES

"Keep the tissues box nearby as you read *True Blue SEALs: Zak* by Sharon Hamilton. I imagine more than I wish to that the circumstances surrounding Zak and Amy are all too real for returning military personnel and their families. Ms. Hamilton has put us right in the middle of struggles and successes that these two high school sweethearts endure. I have read several of Sharon Hamilton's military romances but will say this is the most emotionally intense of the ones that I have read. This is a well-written, realistic story with authentic characters that will have you rooting for them and proud of those who serve to keep us safe. This is an author who writes amazing stories that you love and cry with the characters. Fans of Jessica Scott and Marliss Melton will want to add Sharon Hamilton to their list of realistic military romance writers." (5 Star Review)

"Dear FATHER IN HEAVEN,

If I may respectfully say so sometimes you are a strange God. Though you love all mankind,

It seems you have special predilections too.

You seem to love those men who can stand up alone who face impossible odds, Who challenge every bully and every tyrant ~

Those men who know the heat and loneliness of Calvary. Possibly you cherish men of this stamp because you recognize the mark of your only son in them.

Since this unique group of men known as the SEALs know Calvary and suffering, teach them now the mystery of the resurrection ~ that they are indestructible, that they will live forever because of their deep faith in you.

And when they do come to heaven, may I respectfully warn you, Dear Father, they also know how to celebrate. So please be ready for them when they insert under your pearly gates.

Bless them, their devoted Families and their Country on this glorious occasion.

We ask this through the merits of your Son, Christ Jesus the Lord, Amen."

By Reverend E.J. McMalhon S.J. LCDR, CHC, USN
Awards Ceremony SEAL Team One
1975 At NAB, Coronado